Also by Stephen Wunderli
The Blue Between the Clouds

THE HEARTBEAT OF HALFTIME

THE HEARTBEAT OF HALFTIME

STEPHEN WUNDERLI

HENRY HOLT AND COMPANY • NEW YORK

Henry Holt and Company, Inc.
Publishers since 1866
115 West 18th Street
New York, New York 10011

Henry Holt is a registered
trademark of Henry Holt and Company, Inc.

Published in Canada by Fitzhenry & Whiteside Ltd.,
195 Allstate Parkway, Markham, Ontario L3R 4T8.

Library of Congress Cataloging-in-Publication Data
Wunderli, Stephen.
The heartbeat of halftime/ Stephen Wunderli.
p.   cm.
Summary: Thirteen-year-old Wing clings to the dream that his perpetually losing football team can ride an unexpected winning streak to the championship game before his
father dies of cancer.
[1. Football—Fiction. 2. Fathers and sons—Fiction. 3. Death—Fiction.] I. Title.
PZ7.W96375He   1996   [Fic]—dc20   95-26695

ISBN 0-8050- 4713-1

First Edition—1996

Printed in the United States of America
on acid-free paper. ∞
1   3   5   7   9   10   8   6   4   2

For years, my father was up early on autumn Saturdays to watch two of his sons play football. And sometimes, to coach them. Freddy, my older brother, was gifted in every aspect of the game. He blocked. He tackled. He kicked. And he ran—scrambling for touchdowns while defenses grappled at his shifty body, often separating him from shoes, helmet, and fragments of his jersey . . . but rarely knocking him off his feet. I, on the other hand, was perfectly mediocre. So, to assuage my father of any guilt he may be feeling in his golden years for slightly favoring his older, more athletic son, I am dedicating this book to him: Thanks, Pop, for those times you stood shivering at my games, wishing you were at Freddy's. I harbor no bitter feelings of resentment borne of the sibling rivalry you encouraged. Nope, I'm just fine with the fact that you saw only three of my games and hundreds of his, that he always got to sit in the front seat of the car on game days, that he got to wear your favorite number on his jersey; and I'm not upset in the least that he carried on the family nickname, got hot dogs after the game, was always first to get a haircut, new shoes, and the pick of the lunch boxes (I really did want the Jetsons lunch box, even though I said I didn't after he'd already picked it. You didn't know that did you?). ... On second thought, I think I'll just dedicate this book to Mom.

■ ■ ■

In 1993 I helped coach my son's Olympus Titan team of eight- and nine-year-olds. They were by far the smallest bunch of kids in the league, yet by some miracle, and lots of guts and determination, they won the championship. This book is also for them:

Tyler Beisel	Casey Evans
Taylor Bohling	Junior Fonua
Tyson Bohling	Justin Green
Valan Campbell	Cooper Johnston
Daniel Coya	Nicholas Jones
Kevin Dahle	Joey King
Richard Edman	Parker Lindsay

Richard Lindsay   Jeff Robinson
Anthony Morris   Nicholas Sorensen
Joseph Mortenson   Matt Springer
Chase Nelson   Robbie Swenson
Dustin Porter   Nate Taylor
Richard Prescott   Jonathan Thorne
Michael Rice   Kade Walton
Tyler Rice   Matthew Wunderli

THE HEARTBEAT OF HALFTIME

wanted to start this story back before everything got bad with my pop. Maybe way back to that Saturday morning when he loaded me into his old Buick, told my mother he was off to the hardware store, and, instead, signed me up to play football for the first time in my life. That was three years before Taco Bell banged his head on the wrench shelf in his pop's garage and had a vision of playin' for the Minnesota Vikings; before Heat had any thoughts about livin' with his brother in Alabama and never playin' football again; and before any of us even knew Spray Can. But Spray Can said it wouldn't be right to start back that far on account that he wouldn't be in it, and he likes to be in things from the beginning to the end or not at all. That's how he is. So I won't start with Pop, or Heat, or Taco Bell. I won't even start with our initiation of Sparky, how Heat had puppies in his basement that would squirt out little smelly puppy piles that covered the floor like land mines, and how we made Sparky take off his shoes and socks and find his way out of that basement with the lights off. I won't tell you all that 'cause Spray Can wasn't there to see any of it, 'specially Sparky's toes and in-between all oozin' with yesterday's stinky puppy chow.

I got a whole closet full of notes, some pages of our playbook, and some words I wrote on paper I got from the first girl I ever got a kiss from. Coach put an edit to the whole thing when I got it written, and before that, Spray Can sat with me for a whole Saturday puttin' the scraps and notes in piles to make it chronological. That's when we talked about a beginning.

We decided a good start would be that first day of practice, the first day any of us saw Spray Can. It was almost the end of summer. Heat's dogs were near grown up and sat in the shade watching us on the hot field. Spray Can got there late and was standin' in his torn-out jeans and wearin' no underwear or shirt, waitin' his turn to get his football pads. He never wore socks, not on that first day, and not even when it turned cold. He was standin' right in front of me and the first thing I notice is a long black oil stain across his back.

"You get hit by a car or somethin'?" I asked him.

"No," he said, twistin' his head back to get a look at the slick on his back. "I hadda help Ray thwitch a transthmission before comin' over."

I later found out that Ray was his pop, and although I thought it was funny that he would call his pop by name, what really got me that day was the way he said "switch." His tongue came clear out of his mouth and nearly turned over makin' the *s* sound. It was like it got all confused, flopped out from behind his teeth, and only came to its senses when there was a load of spit hangin' off the tip. Then the word flipped out with the spit and sprayed me on the side of the face. I can't even remember his real name, 'cause from then on we called him Spray Can. I nodded, and didn't wipe off my face till he had turned around. Guess I knew I had a whole season of showers ahead of me, and, well, if Spray Can turned out to be a player, then I didn't want to do anything to discourage him. Lucky for him he did turn out or we'd a put a rag in his mouth right away.

So there we were, the first day of practice, standin' in the heat, puttin' on somebody else's pads, waitin' to get our own sweat on 'em so they'd be ours for sure. We waited while coach checked off our names with each piece of equipment. Then we went into the drills that nobody can do, 'specially the linemen. They're all crammed in pants that hold only half their parts, so stuff is rollin' out everywhere, and they wear huge shoulder pads so their arms don't hardly bend; and they have to run backwards, sideways, on all fours, and through old tires. Looks more like a clown rodeo than a football practice. Then there's the skill positions, guys like me, who are so skinny Coach has to tape our pants on and stuff socks under our shoulder pads. We're the speed and agility of the team. Well, most of us. Some are just plain skinny. We all stumble around like we just learned to walk while Coach shakes his head and kicks us in the butt every time we fall down.

Coach always wore clothes that were twenty or thirty years old. And they were always the same. A white, short-sleeved shirt with a black tie and pants. When it got cold, he threw on an overcoat and a felt hat like detectives wear. His glasses usually hung from his neck by a piece of string and they were always falling apart. So when he talked to us, he was usually putting them back together with a piece of wire or tape. He talked a lot about how it was when he played football. No helmets, no fancy pads. And he looked away a lot, like he was always forgetting something.

Anyway, we were practicin' on a field we had to share with the junior-high school band, and they sounded as bad as we looked. Every now and then the racket they were makin' sounded a little like a melody, but it was drowned out right away by the dyin'-cat sounds they made more often than music. Coach would yell above the moans comin' from the dented instruments, quoting Greek poetry about war and victory and destruction.

"The days of victory pass as the blink of an eye!" he would scream. "But the nights of preparation last forever!"

Then he'd make us all run a lap while he stared up at the mountains in the distance as if the very gods of the universe were watching his handiwork. He always had a cockeyed smile when he stared off like that. It made us think he was either gettin' some kind of answer to his prayers, or he just farted. And maybe that was his answer, because we weren't much of a team.

We'd been together three years, except for Spray Can. And we'd never had a winning season. In fact, we'd won only two games. The first game we won when half the other team was in a car wreck on the way to the game. They stood at the scene of the collision nearly till halftime. By the time they got to the field, we had scored two touchdowns against their six-man defense. The second game we won that same season when the other team's coach was arrested for not payin' child support. It happened in the first quarter; cops drove right onto the field and cuffed him. Kind of rattled his team and we beat 'em by a touchdown. That was the year we began to wonder about miracles.

By the end of our fourth year, the one I'm gonna tell you about, most of the team were believers of the truest sort; some even had sacred charms, like a piece of turf from the university's practice field, or a roll of toilet paper from the same store they say Vince Lombardi stopped at to ask directions on his way through Utah. It was the year of one of the greatest miracles ever witnessed by a football team, or any team, or any person. It was the year of the "holy transformation," as Coach would tearfully say after the last game. "The year the hands of the great football god gathered together an unwitting band of heathens and transformed them into football disciples." It's not how I would've said it, but when it was over, even I knew we'd never see another season like it. "I have only been a tool, an instrument in the hands of a higher power," Coach went on to say; then he walked off toward the mountains and we haven't seen him since.

But on that first day, that first practice, he was nothing more than an old English teacher with a megaphone and a clipboard. Word is he taught somewhere in the Midwest before comin' to Utah to retire and fulfill his lifelong dream of coaching football. We didn't have many dreams that early in the season, so we adopted his. He had this dream of winning. It was a dream we had given up long before we met him. I don't think we even knew what it meant, or what we would have to give up to have it. Pop said, "Winning is the greatest feeling in the world." But he didn't say it until he was sure we weren't losers anymore. Pop always was careful about what he said. Mostly he just threw me the ball, showed me how to hold my hands, cut to the outside. And when he couldn't throw anymore, he talked with his hands. He had big hands that fanned out like a bird, that would wrap slow around a ball. He knew football, my pop did. Better than anyone else I ever knew.

So that first practice we finally get through the equipment and the push-ups and the lectures on discipline and the agility drills, and start to scrimmage. By then, the band had given up trying to carry a tune and march at the same time, so they were just marching like broken wind-up toys back of the end zone. We had banged heads for a few plays and Coach wanted to throw the ball a bit, see what we had. I lined up wide in the backfield to run the deep post, Flame lined up even wider, and we crossed a few yards out to shake the D-backs. It always worked too: The D-backs would stutter-step and we'd gain a yard or so on 'em. Then Bam would drift a wobbly spiral deep for me or Flame to run under and it was six points, at least in scrimmage. Well, bein' the first practice, the D-backs didn't have their feet yet and they crashed right into each other. Flame was laughin' so hard he cut his route short. That left me all alone running for the end zone. Bam launched one that seemed to hang forever while I raced under it. And just as it was about to drop safely into my arms like a loaf of bread, I tripped over a resting clarinet player and plowed headlong into the mute and spastic band.

It took some time to pull myself out of the tuba. I had to take my helmet off first, then wrench it free with the help of Flame, who was still laughing. Taco Bell showed up to help, then Bam, Heat, and finally Spray Can.

"I always wanted to be in the band," he sprayed. "I sthwear."

THE BEGINNING OF A LONG SEASON

We walked home the long way that day, wonderin' to ourselves if we would win a game that season, or if we'd have to suffer through every single Monday lunch period as the garbage dump. See, we were all in the eighth grade. That meant we still had to eat lunch with Ed Stebbings. Fat Ed was in our same league, an Olympus Titan too, but he played for the team a year older. So I guess it bugged him when any Titan team didn't win. All last year he'd bombed our lunch table with mashed potatoes, carrot Jell-O, and drippy ice cream every time we lost. Seems we spent the whole autumn sitting in someone else's leftover lunch.

"I guess Fat Ed'll be back," Flame said.

We all looked down at our feet then, or at the canal we were walkin' beside. The canal moved slow and stinky. It was full of leeches, and sometimes in the summer we'd play war on the banks, throwin' huge stones in the smelly water tryin' to splash each other, or we'd gather rotten produce from the grocery store and fire that at each other like great moldy bombs; but never during football season. When the season began we gave up the wars and saved our fight for the games. Even though we were losers, we still loved the game and fought each one as if we had a chance. And when we lost, we suffered the lunchroom barrage with dignity.

"He'll be back," said Bam. "And he'll be bigger . . . *bam!* . . . just like that."

"Least I got a ice cream last year," Taco Bell said.

We all looked at him, tryin' to figure out what he was talkin' about.

"I got a ice cream when Ed threw it at me. It was only half gone and it landed on a clean part of my shirt, so I ate it."

We all laughed. Taco Bell will eat anything. And if there isn't any food around, he picks at his own scabs and nibbles on them. More than once we've caught him at it, and the only answer he ever has is, "Well, I'm hungry." Then he chews away like there's nothing wrong with it.

"It was good, too," he said about the ice cream. "It was!"

We started shoving him then and someone got

the idea to push him into the canal. But he was big, and he took us all on like a madman.

"I can't get wet!" he screamed. "I have to go to my piano lesson!" That made us try even harder, but it was no use. We finally gave up when Spray Can and Taco Bell knocked heads. Taco Bell didn't notice much, but it raised a lump on Spray Can's eyebrow large enough to hang a dish towel on. Spray Can just sat down and instead of crying about it he let us all watch it grow.

"Wow," said Taco Bell. "It's as big as a peach . . . with ice cream!"

Even Spray Can laughed then and we all walked home after decidin' that if Ed Stebbings and his fellow food throwers started in again this year we'd stand Taco Bell out front to gobble up any incoming. Taco Bell seemed willing enough, so we left it at that, not thinking about it again until we lost our first game.

When I got home, my father was asleep in the chair by the window. Mom was gone, and he kinda half stirred when I shut the door.

"That you, Wing?" he said sleepily. Even Pop called me by my nickname. Maybe he expected me to grow into it.

"Yeah, it's me, Pop," I said.

"How was the first practice?" he said, lifting his head off his shoulder to look at me.

"It was okay, I guess."

"It's too early to tell," he said, trying to smile. "Could be, could be a good year."

"Yeah, right. Is there dinner?" I asked, changing the subject and heading for the kitchen.

"Your mom left you a sandwich in the fridge. I wanted to come by, you know. The first practice is always fun to watch. I, I was just too tired. Sorry."

"It's okay," I said. "You didn't miss much."

I found the sandwich then and went in to sit by Pop. I told him about the man-eating tuba, and about Coach's speeches and this new kid Spray Can. I told him almost everything that happened at practice because I know how much he loves football. He played in college, not a lot because he had a bad hip from a collision in a high-school game. So by the time he got to college, his best years on the field were already spent. He must've wanted to play one more season so bad, but just couldn't.

"I'm the fastest on the team this year, Pop," I said.

"I thought Heat was faster than you."

"Not this year," I said, trying not to be too proud. "I got him by a whole stride."

"Well," Pop said, rubbing the side of his face 'cause it needed a shave. "You have grown; that happens. You're still awful skinny."

"Don't matter," I said, laughing. "They can't hit me if they can't catch me."

Pop agreed, and we both laughed about it. Then I

told him how big Taco Bell had gotten and he wasn't surprised about that at all. He's seen Taco Bell eat too. We would've kept talkin' until Mom got home, but Dad was pretty tired. I helped him out of his chair and he said maybe I was stronger than I looked. He limped off to bed then and I sat down in his chair and looked out the window, looked out at the dark the way he would and wondered what it would be like to wait for a boy to come home from football practice, wait to see him walk up the drive, wait to see him wave, wait for him to come through the door, wait for the cancer to take my body away from it all and leave nothing but an empty chair in an empty room. I think that's when it was hardest, the first few weeks after we found out how short a time he had left with us. Maybe not even as long as a football season.

3
MAYBE WE SHOULD
JOIN THE BAND

For the first three weeks it felt like it would be the longest season in history. We learned fourteen plays, and we did them over and over and over again on the hot, dusty field. And there was the band, always moaning in a sad way, clanging together and stumbling, never moving in one precise motion like bands are supposed to. They were like us. Bumping into each other, trying to learn how to march and play at the same time, trying hard to be a team. They complained, we complained. And when the practice was over we all sat together in the shade of a dying elm tree and waited for our parents to pick us up or for the energy to come back to our muscles so we could walk home. We were an odd bunch then; I think we all felt like misfits. The band that nobody wanted to hear, the football team that no one came to watch. It was kinda funny in a way, because somehow it made us friends.

The first two games were the worst I'd ever seen, or played. We didn't score, we didn't stop anyone from scoring, and the band played the national anthem so badly most folks didn't even know what they were playing. After the second loss, when we were all sitting together under that elm tree after a long Monday practice, Coach walked over and stood in front of us. He didn't bother stepping out of the sun; he just stood there and looked at us for a long time: the band, the football team.

"Well," he finally said, looking at the drummers and horn players. "If we lose another game, why don't you trade places with these guys in pads?"

Some of them kinda laughed. Farts and Fats looked at each other. They were twins. Farts played football with us, and his brother played the tuba. They looked at each other as if to say, "Sure, why not?" Maybe some of the other guys were thinking that same thing, that we might as well trade places. But most of us sat there wondering if we could ever win on our own. Not because of a car accident, or police intervention, but because we earned it. I guess we had lost so many games we had gotten used to it, we expected it. We expected to show up, make a few tackles, run a few plays, watch the other team celebrate, and go home. We expected to go to school the next day, sit at our lunch table, the garbage dump, and have garbage rain down on us like we deserved it.

We sat under the tree for a long time that day. Bam, Taco Bell, Spray Can, Heat, and me. We wanted to change things somehow. But none of us could think of a way to do it. We just looked at each other, looked away, and waited for something to happen. But nothin' did, and we all finally went home.

SPRAY CAN'S LESSON

Bam came over later that night. He must've been thinkin' about it for some time, because it was late and my dad and mom had already gone to bed. I was lyin' there, sorta half asleep. I'd been readin' about the Green Bay Packers, about Vince Lombardi and how he taught them football, how they learned to win, when I heard somethin' hit my window. I woke up, and for a moment I was standing there on the frozen field in Green Bay. Then I heard it again. I looked out the window and I saw, barely visible in the moonlight, Bam, Heat, and Taco Bell surrounded by Heat's dogs.

"What are you doin'?" I said.

"C'mon," they said back. "Get down here, we got someplace to go."

"Whcrc?"

"Just get down here before your folks wake up and . . . *bam!* . . . we're all in trouble."

I pushed the screen out. It was bent from bein' pushed out so many times and it came out easy. Then I walked along the eve and dropped down into the bushes with my shoes in my hand. While I put 'em on, Bam told me what was up.

"We don't know Spray Can," he said.

"Yeah we do," I said.

"We don't," Bam said. "We gotta know him better. The rest of us have been together a long time. Spray Can's got to catch up if we're ever gonna be a team."

I knew he was right. Spray Can had just moved down from Idaho and had never played before. Coach put him at middle linebacker because he could hit. In fact, Spray Can loved to hit, loved to knock people down. But he had a hard time findin' the ball carrier. If it was a sweep, Spray Can would crash the middle. If it was up the middle, Spray Can was poundin' the end. Half the time he was knockin' over his own guys. If we could get him a nose for the ball, get him some smarts, maybe it would make a difference.

We were up and joggin' then, out toward the freeway that rumbled on like a river, day and night. We never paid much attention to it during the day, but at night it seemed more alive. Maybe 'cause nothin' else was goin' on and it was dark. We rested underneath it, feeling the trucks rumble above us. It was like we were beneath the surface of the earth, in a world all our own.

A car turned off a side street and drove toward us. We scrambled up the concrete hill and hid in the shadows. The car stopped and a guy and his girlfriend got out. The car radio was on loud and they started dancing, right there alone, without a band, or friends, or nothin'. We watched for a moment, none of us sayin' anything, just Heat's dogs panting in the dark. Dancin' with a girl had seemed so far away, like none of us would ever do it. Suddenly it was right there. We all knew it was somethin' we'd have to do, that our time was gettin' close. The ninth graders always had a dance at the end of the year and invited the eighth graders. We knew this like we knew about the end of the world. It was a day we feared more than any game day. We watched that couple with a kind of sick fascination, like watchin' a car accident or a house burn down. That is, except for Taco Bell. He had this silly grin on his face like he was enjoying it, like he was looking forward to dancing with a girl. None of us could understand it. When we'd had enough, we snuck away, no one sayin' a word but all of us scared for the future.

None of us knew for sure where Spray Can lived. We knew that his pop owned a gas station up on the boulevard. That was about all we needed to know, because the boulevard is pretty deserted. It's just a highway that runs along the edge of the mountain on the way to the canyon. We also figured that there must be a house close to the station, 'cause that's the direction Spray Can headed every day after practice. We were right. There was only one gas station on the deserted street, and it had a house attached to it. There were no lights on, except for a blue light comin' from a small window in the back. When we got closer we saw that it was the light from the TV. Spray Can was asleep on the couch and a monster movie was playin'. We watched it for a minute. The giant creature from the sea was ripping out telephone poles and stomping on cars. It looked pretty real except for the cars; you could tell they were toys even from where we were watching. Then the creature picked up an ice-cream truck and emptied it. Taco Bell cheered.

"C'mon," Bam said. "We gotta get Spray Can."

The window was small, and it was open. We could see Spray Can's face snoring on the couch.

"Spray Can!" I whispered. "Spray Can, get up."

"Not too loud," Bam said. "We don't want his pop after us."

"He won't wake up," I said.

Taco Bell started rummaging around then. He found a long piece of pipe and handed it to me. I carefully poked it through the window to try and reach Spray Can's shoulder. But it wasn't long enough and all I could reach was his face. I was tryin' to gently tap him on the head, but the pipe was heavy, and, well, it came down pretty hard on his nose.

"Ow!" Spray Can yelped, sitting straight up.

"Spray Can, get up!" Bam whispered.

"What's goin' on?" Spray Can yelled. Then he called his dog. "Bob, come here, boy. Get over here."

Bob was a dirty, mean-lookin' boxer with crooked ears and fierce eyes. He bounded into the room and leaped right for the window, barking crazy, like he wanted to tear us apart.

"Who's out there?" Spray Can yelled.

By then we had fallen over each other and were scrambling through the greasy trash tryin' to get outta there. Heat's dogs went crazy barking and jumping up at the window.

"Who is it?" Spray Can demanded.

"It's us," Taco Bell finally answered. "It's Taco Bell . . . and, and Bam . . . and Wing and Heat."

Spray Can pulled his dog back and looked out the window at the four of us picking our-selves up.

"What are you doin'?"

"We came to talk to you," Bam said. "Where's your pop?"

"He's gone," Spray Can said. "He had to go up to Idaho to pick up a differential. He won't be back till tomorrow."

"He left you alone?" Taco Bell asked.

"Yeah," Spray Can answered casually. "He always does. Go around to the front and I'll open the door."

Spray Can's place was like you'd a thought it to be from the outside: a gas station. He opened the garage door and Bob came running out, but once he saw he was outnumbered, he just stood nervously and let Heat's dogs sniff him. He returned the sniffs and it seemed like everything was okay. Inside the garage there were parts and tools everywhere. In the hallway outside his room there was a small fridge, a hot plate, and a coffee maker.

"Anybody want coffee?" he offered.

No one did. We just stood there looking at all the junk and rags and calendars with girls in bikinis on them. I wondered what a girl that looked like that would want to do with tools, but I don't think it occurred to Taco Bell. He couldn't take his eyes off a skinny blonde holding a muffler and wearin' nothin' but her nightclothes, and there wasn't much of those.

"Wow," Taco Bell said. "Does she work here?"

"'Course she does," Spray Can said. "Why do you think that picture's there for?"

Taco Bell was speechless. For weeks after that he bugged us to get back to Spray Can's during the day. When we finally did go back, he was more disappointed than a kid who's found nothin' in his stocking at Christmas time.

"It was a good game you played Saturday," Bam finally said. "You knocked over lots of people . . . *bam!*"

"Yeah," said Heat. "Some of 'em were even on the other team."

Heat doesn't have much patience for losin'. He's always been a good running back without a line. It's hard to win games by yourself.

"Guess I was kinda confused some of the time," Spray Can said, feelin' bad about the game.

"Well, that's why we're here," Bam said. "We think you hit awful hard. If we could just get you to hit the right player, well . . . *bam!* . . . we think you could be good."

"Really?" asked Spray Can.

"Yeah, really," said Taco Bell.

"We wouldn't be here if we didn't think so," said Bam. "Get me, get me some of them lug nuts and bolts."

Spray Can hurried over to a pan of bolts and brought back a handful. Bam set 'em up like an of fense then set a bolt for Spray Can in the middle of the defense.

"Okay, so here you are," said Bam. "Right in the middle. That means you gotta make most of the tackles. To do that, you gotta know where the ball is goin'. So who's gonna tell you that?"

"I don't know," Spray Can answered. "I just kinda go, you know. . . ."

"That don't work," Bam said. "You gotta watch the line. See, running backs don't like to run alone. They like lots of company in front of 'em. So watch the guards, here and here."

Bam pointed to the two lug nuts that were the offensive guards.

"See, if they back up, it's a pass. If they fire left, it's a run left, right it's a run right."

"Then," said Heat. "You gotta look for the ball carrier. He's usually behind the other back headed the same direction as the guards. Except on the counters and reverses."

"Right," said Bam. "We'll show you."

Bam set up an offense then, with Taco Bell as the center and guard, and me and Heat as the running back. We walked through it first, Taco Bell heading left, me takin' the fake, and Heat gettin' the ball, which was a knot of rags. When we started pickin' up the speed, we ran out of space pretty quick, so Spray Can opened the garage door and pulled out a few of the cars to make more room. He didn't think much of it, but we were all pretty much amazed at watchin' him drive. He said he done it all the time to help out Ray.

Anyway, with more room, we worked on the pass, the fake, the dive, the draw. Spray Can caught on pretty fast. Once he tackled Heat into a pile of empty oil-can boxes. Heat didn't say anything about that. I'd a thought he'd jump up and tell Spray Can to save the hits for the game. But he didn't. He smiled like a proud father, then went back to running plays.

It was pretty late when we finished. We were havin' a good time, more fun than we'd had on the football field for a long time. It made us remember why we played football in the first place: 'cause it was fun.

"You're gettin' it," Bam said to Spray Can. "Too bad Ray ain't here."

"Wouldn't matter," Spray Can said.

"What do you mean?" I asked him.

"Just wouldn't matter, that's all."

I didn't know what he was talkin' about until the next game, when I looked around for Ray and didn't find him. Seems Ray had no interest in Spray Can at all.

We left Spray Can and his dog Bob all breathin'

hard from the game that night. Bob was as tired as any of us 'cause he was so old. He couldn't muster up a bark when we walked out the door. It was past midnight, but we weren't sleepy. We took the rag ball with us and tossed it all the way home, laughin' and scorin' touchdowns. Maybe we even dreamed of winning. Maybe.

HEAT'S WAY

Anyone who didn't know Heat the way we did said he was better with dogs than he was with people. He never said a whole lot, and what he did say wasn't exactly pleasant. Heat had a mother who didn't like children. So when she had one, she didn't act like she did. Oh, she was nice enough, but she never spent a lot of time with Heat. She just kind of let him go off and do what he pleased. So maybe Heat never got what he needed from his mother. Maybe he wanted her to be around a bit more, or talk to him, or just plain take an interest in him. But she didn't. She ignored him. So Heat spent most of his time with his dogs, four black Labradors. They were beautiful in the sun, their fur shiny and thick. And Heat was with them so much that they were almost human. He talked to them like they were his family. He could send one to the store for a bag of Oreos, while another bought movie tickets. They were that smart.

You never saw Heat without his dogs. Most of the time he was jogging along with his pack. Sometimes, when he was short of money, he'd jog through town with an old flour sack. He'd send the dogs up and down the alleys collecting bottles. I guess that's what made him so fast, running with his dogs all the time. You could knock his feet out from underneath him and he'd put a hand down for balance, twist in the air, and be back on his feet at full gallop. I guess he learned a lot from those dogs. Heat had his own way, and he was the only one of us Ed Stebbings wouldn't touch.

The way Heat tells it, the story goes like this: He was out collecting bottles one day and it got kinda late. He was headed home beside the canal when he ran into Lance Lindsay, Ed's bud, and a few of his friends. The dogs were off lookin' for bottles and Heat was alone on the path.

"Well, if it ain't the running back for the girl's team," Lindsay said, and I'm sure his brainless teammates laughed then.

"We could use some cheerleaders," he said. "We think you and the rest of the girls on your team would be perfect."

Heat didn't say anything. He never does.

"Well?" said Lindsay.

Heat just stood there.

"Give us an answer, pansy, or we'll throw you in the canal."

Heat was probably pretty mad about this time. But he has a hard time findin' the right words. So mostly he keeps his mouth shut.

Right here's where I should tell you about one of the tricks Heat taught his dogs. I don't know how he did it, but he taught them all to lunge for the zipper. So on command, any one of these four dogs would head-butt you right below the belt. And they could punch so hard with those stiff snouts that it didn't matter if you had a cup on. You felt it. He tried it on me one day after practice and I thought I'd been hit by a baseball.

Anyway, Lindsay kept after Heat there at the canal. "What's it gonna be, wimp?" Lindsay said in a squeaky voice. "You wanna put a wig on and watch the big boys play, huh?"

Well, they must've been laughin' real hard then, 'cause they didn't hear Heat whistle for his dogs. It was dark and pretty hard to see three black dogs trotting up from behind Heat. The fourth one was across the canal, and when he splashed in, Lindsay and his two buddies looked over to see what was comin' out of the water. What they didn't see was three black Labs running full speed with their snouts in the ram position. The dogs struck enemy crotches like invisible missiles.

One thing was for certain that night: Neither Lindsay or his buds were wearing cups. They fell to the ground like, well, like they had been socked right in the goods. They lay there for some time while the dogs stood snarling above them. Heat never said a word. He just walked off down the path with his pack of dogs scouting out in front of him, looking for bottles or crotch targets, whatever they could find.

Anyway, that's why Ed never messes with Heat. By the time he got the story from Lindsay, they had made Heat out to be some kind of crazyman who lived with a pack of wolves. No, you never see Heat without his dogs. It's like they're family, brothers, I guess. Heat's spent so much time with his dogs, some people say it's given him strange ways. Maybe the strangest is Heat's habit of jogging to the football field the night before a game to mark his territory in the end zone. See, dogs will pee on every corner. It's their way of letting other dogs know where their territory is, letting them know they got a fight comin' if they cross the line. It's like layin' claim to a piece of ground, sayin' this is mine. So Heat does it the night before each game. Sometime after midnight he jogs down to the field with his dogs. And then in some kind of ceremonial way, he pees in each end zone. It's his way of saying, "The only one who can score here is me." I never would have known it, but the night before our third game I couldn't sleep. So I got up and sat on my roof like I always do when I can't sleep. I could see over to the other street because there was a full moon out; and I see this pack of dogs moving up the sidewalk. At first I thought it was just a bunch of strays out sneakin' around at night. Then I notice their tight formation, and Heat running right behind them. I only had to watch for a moment, and I knew where he was going.

I climbed down and followed him. I watched him run to the far goalpost and pee while his dogs waited for him. I walked into the other end zone and just stood there. He turned and trotted toward me. He didn't see me until he was almost to the twenty. I think I scared him, but he didn't act like it.

"What are you doin'?" I asked him.

He didn't answer; he just looked at me, tryin' to figure out if he could trust me or not. Finally he spoke up.

"Move," he said. "You're in my way."

I stepped aside and stood with the dogs while he marked the end zone. He went on like it was the most logical thing to do, that it was a part of nature, a kind of force that would drive away our enemies. He said that there was something primitive about it and that we needed all the help we could get.

"I guess so," I said. Then I marked my own territory just inside the goal line. Heat didn't say anything about it, just nodded his head in approval. Even the dogs seemed to be smiling, like they had taught us some great truth. Maybe they had.

THE FORCES OF NATURE

ature is a funny thing. When you think it makes the most sense, it changes course. Yeah, we lost. It was the first game I really thought we had a chance of winning. We had a good week of practice. Coach even said that we were wakin' up like the Greek statue Colossus, all bronze and ten stories high. Slowly it came to life, breakin' out of its bronze skin to destroy the centurions.

"Football is a thinking man's game," Coach said over and over. "Intelligence is the finest weapon in the arsenal. Think, think, think."

And we did. Spray Can would screw up his face whenever he was figurin' somethin' like when's the best time to blitz, or fall back, or shade left or right. He was gettin' it. So when we stood there in the cool morning air early on game day goin' through our stretches and warm-ups, all I could think of was eating my lunch in peace . . . walking through the lunchroom with a tray in my hands and not hearing a word, sitting at a table like I was at a restaurant, slowly eating, laughing, retelling football stories, stories of great victories. I was prepared to win. I had worked hard. I had marked my territory.

But the stories would have to wait just a little bit longer, wait because Heat would fumble on the three yard line with two minutes left in the game and the mighty Titans would lose by one point. One point! Still, it was a good game. We all knew it. Spray Can had seven tackles. He knew where the ball was most of the time, he tackled so hard even the referees closed their eyes whenever he hit someone. He hit their halfback so hard on a sweep it sent the poor kid skidding out of bounds and onto the gravel track without his helmet on. That was the kind of day he was having. And our offense was scoring. Not once, but twice. The first time, Bam pulled off a fake to Heat and slipped me the ball on the counter. Nobody knew I even had the ball. Then Heat ran a punt back for a touchdown to give us ungodly confidence. Bam went for the extra point on a sneak, but came up short. So when "the jaws of hell opened up," as Coach said after the game, we were down by only one. We drove the ball the length of the field on our last possession. The guards were playing like madmen, pounding the defense back every time the ball was snapped. Then, on the last play, the 38 power pitch, Bam delivered the ball to Heat in mid stride, Taco Bell pulled from the guard slot and blasted the outside linebacker into the band on the sidelines. Heat cut the corner and the free safety came crashing in. We knew Heat could run over him, could pound him, dodge him, even drag him for three yards if he had to. We were cheering before they even collided. Heat went right through him, like kicking his way through a door. He was standing up in the end zone before he realized the little bullet had punched the ball loose. We all watched in horror as the ball bounded away from us, bounced slowly like someone had dropped it on the way to school. Then a red jersey—not a green jersey, not one of ours, but a red one, a bright red jersey like the light on an ambulance—landed on the ball. The skinny cornerback cradled it like a pot of gold while we all piled on. But it didn't matter. In a few plays the gun would sound, the game would be over, and we would still be losers. We would still walk away from the football field as losers while the other team celebrated. We would still have to sit in the garbage dump. Of all the losses in our football lives, that one was by far the hardest. All Heat could say after the game was that he should've moved to Alabama.

I was so caught up in the game that I didn't see my father leave early. He had stumbled on the sideline, too weak to pull himself up. Mom took him to the hospital for a day's worth of tests and drugs. When I finally did see him, he was in his chair with a blanket around his legs, staring out the window again. Staring like he was waiting for somebody again. I sat beside him and lifted a glass of water close enough so he could sip from the straw. That's when I told him we lost.

"We couldn't beat 'em," I said. "We just couldn't. It was there in front of us, but still we lost it. I don't know why."

Pop told me he knew how I felt. He had lost his share of games in his life. Then he said the fight was more important than the outcome. But I think he still would've rather seen me win that day. It made me mad to think about him sitting there, not being able to toss me the ball the way he used to. I was pretty small when I first started playing football, so my pop taught me to catch. Every day after school I'd wait for him to come home and throw me the ball. I'd throw the ball on the roof and dive for it as it came rolling off. Throw it again, and wait. Throw it again, and wait. Finally Pop would get home and set his briefcase down on the driveway and toss me passes in his suit and tie. I'd run post patterns, flags, up-and-ins, down-and-outs, curls, flashes. . . .

I sat there with him, looking out at the grass where we used to play. I could see the bushes in one end zone and the low fence behind it.

"Remember when you threw me a bomb, Pop," I whispered to him. "And . . . and I dove over the fence to make the catch, remember?"

But he was already asleep. I tucked the blanket in around his legs and went to bed.

7

THE GARBAGE DUMP

We must've all been thinkin' the same thing that next Monday at lunchtime. We stood by the candy machines, holding our lunch trays and staring at our table. It was empty 'cause we were all standing, waiting. No one would sit down. We looked over at Ed Stebbings's table. It was full. They were laughing, paying no attention to us because they had won. But we knew they were waiting, waiting for us to sit down like slow-moving targets.

"I'm hungry," Taco bell said.

Nobody answered him.

"Well?" Taco Bell said, trying to look each of us in the eye. We all looked at our lunches, wondering what they would look like splattered on our heads. It had to be spaghetti that day. And pears, there were those pear halves, and green Jell-O and a hard brownie with sticky frosting. "That frosting will be hard to wash off," I remember thinking. Spray Can walked up with two extra milks and an extra helping of the gross spaghetti that looked like fish bait.

"Let's go," he said.

"Yeah," Bam said. "Might as well take what's comin' to us."

Slowly we walked over to the dumping grounds and sat down. We all looked at each other, our eyes kinda half squinted like we were waiting to get hit. But it didn't come. We waited like prisoners in front of a firing line, picking at our last meal. Finally, Ed Stebbings walked up and put his hand on Taco Bell. Taco Bell about jumped out of his chair.

"What? What do you want?" he screamed.

"Chill it, fat boy," Ed said. "We just came over to say you guys played a good game yesterday."

"You did, I mean, we did?" Taco Bell stammered.

"Yeah," Ed continued. "You played a great game . . . but you still lost."

And with that, Ed clapped a pear half on Taco Bell's head, syrup and all. Then they all laughed and tossed milk cartons and sacks at us. Taco Bell tried to laugh, but I could tell he felt real bad, like he was about to cry. He had played his heart out and still lost. I don't think I've ever seen him so hurt. He just sat there, shaking like his whole life was ending.

"You're a jerk!" I said to Ed Stebbings.

The whole lunchroom went dead silent, like I'd said the worst string of bad words or body parts I could think of. Nobody ever said anything back to Ed. He was big, and he had red hair that made him look like he was mad all the time. He never brushed his teeth and he loved to pull smaller kids into headlocks and tell them what crybabies they were, with that stinky breath all over their faces. Once he caught a mouse and killed it by squashin' it in his hand. He was that mean. He just looked at me, kinda smiled wickedly, and punched me in the stomach. By the time I had caught my breath, Fat Ed had emptied three lunch trays on my head and dumped two cans of pop in my left pocket. Then he had me in that headlock and was draggin' me toward the wet-garbage can when the janitor broke it up. It's a good thing, too; that wet-garbage can has caused more than one kid to throw up just from takin' a peek at what's inside. It's where everybody scrapes off their lunch trays before stackin' 'em up to be washed. You could die in there, I swear.

Luckily the janitor was strong, and he was used to bad smells after years of mopping up vomit. It didn't bother him one bit to pick us both up and haul us down to the principal's office. I didn't stay there very long; guess I smelled pretty bad. They called my mom and told me to wait outside until she came for me. I sat out there alone, wondering if it was too late to join the band.

AN ATTITUDE PROBLEM

"**T**his is not amusing," my mother said as we walked out of the principal's office. "I don't know why you insist on embarrassing me this way. You know, I got the call when I was in a meeting. 'Mrs. Hyde, the principal from your son's school is on the phone.' Terrific."

I don't remember the rest of what she said; all I remember is how mad she was. She made me pull off my shirt and pants and put them in the trunk before I could get in her car. I sat in the backseat in my underwear, listening to her tell me how she could now forget about a raise, she'd be the joke of the office, and that it would be a long time before I could make this one up to her. I just sat there, slowly scraping the brown frosting off my face like I was taking off war paint. My hair was full of pear syrup and stuck straight up on top like a Mohawk. I could see myself in the rearview mirror and thought I looked pretty fierce, and I guess I was feeling too much like a warrior who doesn't need his mother.

"I'd do it again," I said.

My mother stopped the car. We were still a few blocks from home. "You'd what?" she said, more than a little upset.

"I'd do it again," I said. "I don't care if they call you every day for the rest of my life."

"You have an attitude problem," she snapped.

"You're the one with the problem," I said without thinking.

"You're right," she said, calming down. "My problem is you."

I guess it's not a real good idea to smart off to your mom when you're a few blocks from home wearin' nothing but your underwear. A mom could come in handy in a situation like that. But I didn't realize it until she was driving away and I was standing in the street, hoping that everybody I knew was either at work or school. As it turns out, I saw only two people. Mrs. Porter, who is nearly blind. She waved to me like she does every day, didn't notice a thing. And the mailman. He walked by quickly, and without missing a stride said, "Must have hippies for parents."

"I wish," I said back to him, walking as fast as I could. I figured if I ran, it would draw attention to me and someone might think there was a fire or some kind of uprising. So I just walked proudly home like the emperor with no clothes. Mom had gone back to the office and Pop was sleeping, so I took a shower and waited for football practice. I went out back and tossed the ball on the roof over and over, not knowing where it would come off and diving for it when it did. I could tell then that I had changed, even before practice started. At first I was just bored and alone. I threw the ball up and caught it. Then I threw it farther away and had to dive to catch it. I'd throw it on the roof and crash through the bushes to make the catch. It was different than it had been before. I wasn't waiting for anyone. I was alone, I figured I would always be alone. Nothing mattered to me except football, it was all I had left. I headed out to practice before my father got up and made his way to his chair. I left before he could wave good-bye to me. I got my pads on and I walked to the field alone. When we scrimmaged that day, I threw blocks that sent the linebackers onto their heads. I caught every pass, and once, on an up-and-in, I caught the ball and instead of jukin' Sparky I ran right over him. We hit helmet to helmet and I knocked him flat on his back. He went and sat down on the side and wouldn't play the rest of practice. "That's football," I said to myself. "That's what it's all about."

"You're playin' like a madman," Bam said in the huddle. "You got somethin' to prove?"

"Yeah," I said. "I do. Throw me the ball."

He did. I caught it, but before I could slam Flash, the free safety, he let up.

"What are you afraid of?" I yelled at him.

"Save it for the game," he said back.

"You save it," I said. "I'm not holdin' nothin' back."

And I didn't. Not that day, not the next two practices. By the time Friday night rolled around, I was ready to punish somebody, anybody, for everything I had lost.

MAKE THE ADJUSTMENT

I wasn't asleep when Heat came by. I was on the roof again and I saw him and his pack of dogs walk onto my front lawn. Bam was with him, and so was Spray Can and Taco Bell. I knew what they were there for.

"It didn't work last time," I said from the roof.

They looked up at me. I was curled up in my blanket and perched on the edge of the roof like some kind of gargoyle.

"We didn't have enough of us," Heat said. "The more we get, the stronger the force will be."

I didn't have anything better to do, so I climbed down and went with them. Truth is I had to go anyway, so it might as well be in the end zone. No one said anything while we walked; I guess they were all thinking about the task at hand, hoping desperately that this would help, that the force of nature would be strong enough to give us the edge we needed to win a game. I had my doubts, but I was willing to try.

When we got to the field, everybody just stood around, nervous, like we were at a dance with girls or somethin'.

"Okay," Heat said, getting right down to business. "We go in both end zones. That way we're the only ones who can lay claim to either, you got it?"

We all nodded our heads like we were about to embark on a top-secret mission.

"Oh," he added. "One more thing. We'll start there, but you got to save some for down here. It doesn't do any good to only do one."

We agreed again, seeing the logic. If we marked only one, well, that meant we'd have only one good half. A team can come back and beat you if you play good ball for only half a game. It made sense to us. But, you know, it was a lot more diffi-cult than it sounded. Think about it. You're goin' in the first end zone; halfway through, you have to shut it off, then run a hundred yards to the other end zone, and let the rest out. It took some practice to get good at it. But we did. By the last game, we could squirt out a little, then walk casually down-field and squirt the rest. We were that good. In fact, we were so good we could mark just about anything, anytime.

When we were done marking, we sat down in the middle of the field and talked about the plays we had learned that week. You see, every team has a little different defense. So even though we had most of our plays learned, we changed 'em just a little bit for each game. We were playing the Woods Cross Warriors the next day. We knew they had some big guys in the middle who would clog up our power plays. So Coach changed our dives to run off tackle instead of off guard. We also changed our sweep a little, pulled the guard from the far side so we had more blocking. See, those big guys are strong, but they're not fast, so we figured we'd run sweeps all day until they stacked the ends, and then we'd run off tackle. If that didn't work, we'd throw the ball.

Bam had a football, he always had a football, and we ran through the plays until it was almost midnight. Heat set up his dogs like the defensive line, and Taco Bell pulled over and over. Bam pitched and handed off to Heat and I ran pass patterns. Since Spray Can only played defense, he covered me every time I went out. On the way home we talked about Woods Cross and what they would throw at Spray Can.

"They got lots of big guys," Bam said. "So they like to run up the middle a lot. You're gonna have to take on two or three blockers at a time . . . *bam* . . . *bam* . . . *bam!* Like that."

"I can do it, I sthwear," Spray Can sprayed.

For the first time that year, we believed him.

SOMETHING TO PROVE

My father gets up early on Saturday mornings. By the time I wake up, my uniform has been washed and dried and he's sitting on the downstairs couch pushing my pads into the pants. There are clean socks beside him, next to my jersey, and a shirt for under the shoulder pads. I always wake up and sit on the fireplace, rubbing my face awake. This is our time, when the house is quiet, to talk about football. If there is anything else that needs to be talked out, it comes later, after the game, after we have talked about each play. And even though most afternoon talks were about a loss, the morning talks were always optimistic. I sat there that morning watching my father tiredly thread the belt through the slits in my pants. His hands were shaking, but it was his job and I didn't want to take it away from him.

When he was done, he was breathing hard and his eyes were half closed and sad.

"Bam will give you a ride this morning," he said. "And I'll try to make it to at least part of the game."

"Okay," I said back to him.

He closed his eyes then and laid his head back on the couch. I got dressed while he breathed through his mouth. His skin had turned pale and I could see the bluish veins running across his face like highways, tiny rivers of traffic running over his cheeks. It made me think of all the places he had been. Oakland, California, where he'd been born. Santa Fe, where he'd worked for a winter, Norfolk in the Navy, Germany on some base there, Missoula with a friend and a broken-down cattle ranch, Salt Lake City selling oil property, our small street—a stream that runs into the main river, with small houses right up to its edge like it's only a matter of time before the water washes them all away.

"Pop," I whispered into his face. "Pop, I'm leavin' now."

He half opened his eyes. "Okay, okay," he said softly. "See you there."

I didn't say much to Bam on the way to the game. His older brother Darrel drove us over to the high school. Darrel was on the high-school football team. He was proud of his little brother and wanted Bam to be a hero like himself. He turned the music up loud and shouted over it.

"You guys are about due for a win," he yelled. "I'd say it's about your turn." Then he'd slug one of us on the shoulder pad or cuff us on the back of the head.

"Are you ready?" he yelled.

"Yeah, we're ready," Bam shouted back when we were climbing out of the car.

"How 'bout you, Wing?" he said to me. "You ready, huh, huh?"

"Shut up," I said. "This isn't your game."

"That's right," Darrel said, after thinking about it for a minute. "I'd make sure I'd win, if it was. You got what it takes to make sure, Wing, huh?"

I didn't say anything back, just walked ahead of him, feeling him staring at me like he wanted to kick me or somethin'.

"What's with you?" Bam said when we were stretching out.

I didn't answer that, either. I was eager to get the game started and I was looking over at the other team, their blue-and-white uniforms jumping up and down in perfect sync like a platoon of soldiers. I wanted to get up right then and run toward them, crash into 'em, send every one of them flying like bowling pins. But I figured my chance would come.

It did, the very first play of the game. We won the flip and would receive. Heat and I lined up deep to take the kick. It sailed in Heat's direction, but I cut in front of him, hauled in the kick, and headed right down the middle. By the time I hit the swarm of blue jerseys, I was running faster than I ever had before. Taco Bell cut in front of me to pick up one of their guys, and I shoved him right into the on-coming traffic. It was a good block, but there was someone else right behind him. I hit this tall kid at full speed and knocked him right onto his butt. Someone hit me from the side, but I stepped through it, then cut to the outside and straight-armed another blue jersey. I picked up speed, head-ing down the sideline right in front of our team. I could hear them screaming, I could see them jump-ing up and down. I could also see the kicker, the last man between me and the goal line. He had the angle on me and was coming fast. I usually would have tried to get lower than him, to hit him hard and get a few extra yards with him rid-ing on my back all the way to the ground. But this time I stayed high. I lowered my head just enough to meet his. We cracked head-on like two rams. *Boom!* He stumbled backward, and I spun off him and sprinted the thirty yards to the goal line. I let the ball drop out of my hands in the end zone, and before the whole team piled on top of me, I caught a glimpse of Darrel. He was wearing a big smile, and I looked at him, telling him, *Yes, I have what it takes. No one gave it to me, and no one is going to take it away.*

I stood by Heat while the defense took the field. It

took him a bit to say something to me, but he finally did.

"We been talkin' about it," he said. "You got something to prove, maybe with your pop, maybe somethin' else. That's good. But you're not the only one."

The next offensive series, Heat ran sixty yards in three carries. He was running like a fugitive, and it took at least three men to take him down each time. Bam called time-out on the seven yard line, and while Coach was jogging out onto the field, Bam grabbed us both by the face masks and smacked our heads together.

"What is it, huh?" he yelled at us. "What is it?"

"We got somethin' to prove," Heat said. "Do you?"

Bam nodded his head.

"What's wrong?" Coach said when he got there. "Somebody hurt?"

"No," Bam said. "I got two backs who are running like freight trains . . . bam . . . bam! Who do I give it to?"

"Fake the sweep left and run the bootleg right," he said. "The whole modern world will follow these two prophets and you'll be the lone sinner standing in the end zone."

Bam smiled. It was his turn to prove something. He had never scored a touchdown, and the thought of it made his whole face light up. I pulled left, Heat took the fake, and we headed for the goal line. Taco Bell pulled and went right, but Bam didn't need him. It was a long moment before anybody, including the referees, knew that Bam had scored. Bam was celebrating with Taco Bell and the refs were sorting out the pile on the other side of the field, trying to figure out who had the ball.

The other coach figured it out and threw his clipboard down and pointed at Bam. Bam just laughed and danced all the way back to our bench. Darrel picked him up when he got there and asked him how it felt.

"I don't ever want to feel anything else," he said.

And we wouldn't, not that day. Spray Can had somethin' to prove too, so the other team never scored. Spray Can was everywhere. He gave us good field position and he got the rest of the defense fired up and sort of crazy like himself. We scored again in the third quarter after Bam hucked me a long pass and I brushed the sideline inside the ten trying to keep my balance. Then Heat pounded his way through the middle and all three of us had TDs. First time ever. When the game was over, we wanted to play another one. Coach was saying something about the Greeks but no one was listening, 'specially me. I was looking around to see if Pop was still there. I saw him earlier, kind of off by himself, leaning heavy on a cane Mom had bought him so he could get around better. But he must not have stayed very long. When I couldn't find him, I walked off, away from the rest of the team. I wanted to be alone. I didn't feel a part of anything. I hadn't won for anybody but myself, and I wanted to keep it that way.

11

THE LEGEND OF
ED STEBBINGS

When the bell rang, we ran all the way to the lunchroom. We were first in line. First to sit down at our table. We spread out like royalty, sharing chicken legs and tossing each other grapes. It was our day, our lunchroom, our table, our trays. Food that we would normally wear was suddenly transformed into a feast for the gods.

"I believe I'll have another piece of chicken," Taco Bell said like the Prince of Wales.

"Yes," Bam said. "It is cooked to perfection, isn't it?"

"Quite lovely," said Flame. "Compliment the chef for me will you, Master Wing?"

"I'll tell him," I said, not wanting to spoil the atmosphere.

A strange silence fell over the lunchroom then.

It took a moment for the others to notice it, but it hit me like a blast of cold wind. And as soon as I felt it, I knew where it came from. Ed Stebbings had just walked in the room. Not a person moved. They all stared at Ed and his gang, waiting. Then the wave of whispers washed across the lunchroom. You could hear the message before it got to you. "They lost," the wave said. "They lost."

We were stunned. We'd never thought to find out if Ed had won on Saturday. He always did. And we were so caught up in our own victory that we didn't care about anything else until we saw him standing there, waiting to get his lunch. He was the inmate now, waiting, staring like an animal, wanting to hurt somebody. The look on his face was so mean, so angry. No wonder the room went deadly silent. Ed wasn't about to cower away from anybody. He gave that look to all of us, one at a time. He dared anyone to say something about the game, about the loss. Nobody would. After he collected his lunch, he sat down with the rest of his angry crew. By now every single eye was turned to him. He sat for a moment, then threw his head in his hands.

"We lost!" he cried. "We lost!"

We were all in shock.

Then he jerked his head up and screamed at us all. "What do you think I am, a crybaby like all of you? We lost a game! So what! Any of you have a problem with that?"

Suddenly, we became very interested in what we were eating.

Ed stood up and walked over to our table. The forks stopped moving, the mouths stopped chewing. No one even breathed.

Ed stood behind Taco Bell.

Taco Bell stared at his green beans. Ed picked up a spoonful of beans and mashed them in Taco Bell's white cake.

"Do you have a problem with the way I played on Saturday?"

Taco Bell just shook his head quickly, like a mouse in the paws of a cat. Ed pushed his face next to Spray Can.

"Do you have a problem?" he said, slowly pouring Spray Can's milk over the chicken.

"No," Spray Can said reluctantly.

Then Ed moved over beside me. He reached slowly for my piece of cake as he began to talk. I held a fork in my hand and stabbed so hard at Ed's hand that the fork bent on the table when I missed him.

"Why you—" he started angrily. But just then the principal walked in.

"Congratulations!" he said to all of us. "You finally won a game. There will be many more wins, I'm sure."

He walked closer and looked at Ed and me together.

"Well," he said. "I guess Ed has come to congratulate you too."

"Yes, he has," I said, and everyone sighed in relief. "Ed just came over here to tell us how good we played, and, and he offered to buy me an ice-cream sandwich."

"Well, that's very nice, Ed," the principal said. "I'm glad I was here to see it. Don't let me stop you."

Ed's face was so tight, I thought it was going to rip apart from the inside out. He somehow forced his mouth into a smile and threw his arm around me.

"That's right," he said. "I'm going to buy my little hero an ice-cream sandwich."

The two of us walked awkwardly to the vending machine. Ed pulled his arm off me so he could find a quarter in his pocket. His hand was shaking, he was so mad. When the ice cream dropped out, he handed it to me like it was an expensive present he spent all day shopping for.

"There you go, champ," he said sarcastically, and patted me on the head. I unwrapped it slowly while he watched me. He was burning inside.

"That's very nice, Ed," the principal said, putting his hand on Ed's shoulder.

While he talked to Ed about being a good sport, I took a nice big bite of that ice-cream sandwich. Ed fumed. His whole body was shaking. The veins on his head were pumping like they were about to burst. I knew as soon as the principal left, mad Ed would grab the ice cream out of my hand, shove it in his mouth, then dunk my head in the wet-garbage can. So when the principal stepped between us to tell Ed what a marvelous human being he was, I looked around until I caught sight of a chunk of chewed gum sticking to a skinny girl's lunch tray. I pulled it off and stuffed it inside the sandwich. The principal finished his speech to Ed, patted me on the shoulder, and walked away. We both stood there, Ed watching the principal and keeping a hand in front of me so I couldn't leave, and me smiling like I was so glad to have a new friend. When the principal was gone, Ed looked at me.

"Give me that!" he sneered, snatching the ice cream from me. "If we weren't in school right now, I'd rip your guts out and stomp you to bits and serve you up to all these losers!"

His arm swept out in front of him, and he had a crazy face like Hitler's in those newsreels they make us watch in history. I just smiled, and Ed the angry dictator chomped down hard on that ice cream. It took a few chews before he found the skinny girl's gum, but I was gone by then, clear out in the hallway, running to my next class. I did hear him yell though. I bet they heard that yell all the way to the football field.

THE HEARTBEAT
OF HALFTIME

don't know how I missed it the first time. Maybe the first win was just too much like a dream. And maybe there are times when you just don't feel anything. So it wasn't until the next game that I discovered the heartbeat of halftime.

Halftime. It's when you take a good look at everything. The stuff that's going right, and the stuff that's going wrong. Then you try to adjust so you're doing more of the stuff that's going right. But see, it's also kind of a quiet time. A time when you can feel your own heartbeat. *Thump* thump. *Thump* thump. Like that. A big beat, a little beat. Each of them has something to say. If you're winning, the big beat tells you so. But then there's that little beat that says maybe you could lose, maybe. There's always that chance. And it's the same when you're losing. The big beat says there's no way to come back, but the little beat says maybe, maybe we can win. *Thump* thump. Like that.

So in the next game, we were behind 7 to 6 at halftime. It was the game Spray Can jammed his thumb and sat out the whole second quarter. When halftime came, we were walking away from the field to talk about what was wrong and what was right that day. I shoved Spray Can, almost knocked him down. I guess I was just mad that he was out of the game.

"They wouldn't a scored if you'd just stayed in," I said to him.

"I jammed my thumb," he sprayed.

"You gave up," I said angrily. "You quit, that's all. You just quit."

"No I didn't," he said.

Then he pushed me, hard.

"You came here to lose," I said, and I pushed him back.

He took a swing at me then with his good hand and hit me just above the eye.

"Loser!" I shouted at him.

He swung again, but missed.

"You got something to prove?" I screamed in his face

"Yeth!" he shouted.

Coach stepped in before Spray Can could swing at me again.

"Prove it!" I yelled at Spray Can. "Prove it!"

Coach didn't say anything then. He just looked at the anger in my eyes, and the hurt in Spray Can's. He grabbed us both by the jerseys and led us to a spot of shade. Then he made everybody sit down and take off his shoulder pads. He still didn't say anything, no speech about the Greeks or Homer, no shouting about victory. He looked at us hard, then pulled the marker off his clipboard and told me to stand up.

"Do you have something to prove, Wing?" he said to me in a quiet voice.

I looked at him, right into his eyes, and said, "Yes."

"Come here," he said.

When I stepped forward, he wrote something on the front of my T-shirt. No one could see what he was writing but me. When he was finished, he looked me in the eyes and said what he had written on my shirt: "Prove it!"

Then he turned me around so everybody could see what he had written.

"Prove it," he said again.

We all nodded our heads, quietly, understanding the message.

"Prove it out there," he said, pointing at the football field. "Prove it every time you touch the football, ever time you block. Every time you step on that field, figure out what it is you have to prove and do it!"

Then he handed the marker to Spray Can, to Heat, to Bam, to Flame, to everyone on the team. And when we were finished, he shouted, "Do you have something to prove?"

"Yes," we shouted back.

"Do you?"

"Yes!"

"Are you losers?"

"No!"

"Then go prove it!"

The second half of that game was a lot different from the first. It wasn't just Heat who had a good game, or Spray Can who played like a madman, or even me. We were like a crazed platoon storming the beach at Normandy. On the opening kickoff we attacked so hard, the ball was knocked loose and we recovered on the twelve yard line. It was like a swarm of madmen, not just one. Bam kicked off and we thundered down the field, yelling like warriors and crashing through blockers like they were made out of cardboard. After recovering the fumble, we scored on the very next play. Bam handed off to Heat on a power play and he ran right over the middle linebacker, then the safety. It was like turning a bull loose and watching him charge through a corn patch.

There was no celebration when Heat scored. He just let the ball drop out of his hand and trotted back to the huddle to get ready for the conversion.

Bam looked at him, then at the rest of us, and called the same play. Heat stepped through the line this time like he was stepping through a curtain for an encore. I almost expected him to take a bow. But he didn't. He jogged back down to midfield to get ready for another kickoff.

Bam boomed the kickoff deep, and the rest was all Spray Can's defense. They'd line up on the ball and Spray Can would jump around, slapping them all on the helmets with his good hand and shouting "Prove it! . . . Prove it right here! . . . Right now!"

And they did. The other team never gained so much as an inch the rest of the game. And our offense was relentless. We scored three touchdowns that second half. Two by ground with Heat, and one by air, to me. It was a deep post, the one we worked on every day at practice, the one I dream about in my sleep, the one I have run a thousand times in my front yard. I ran my pattern and the ball was there, as easily as if we were all sitting down to a picnic and Bam tossed me a sandwich. I didn't break stride. I didn't have trouble hauling the ball in. It just came naturally, like I was born to catch passes.

The band started playing after that touchdown. It was just after the two-minute warning. No one recognized the song they were playing, and the beat didn't seem to match the melody. As I stood on the sideline listening to the band and watching our defense play out the rest of the game, I thought maybe this was all how it should be. Maybe nothing is ever perfect and all you can do is play hard, play it the best way you know how. Even if you're only in the band.

I looked around for my father then. It was the first time I had looked for him all game, even though I knew he wouldn't be there.

"He's too tired," Mom had said before I left the house that morning. "Just too tired to make it to a football game."

LOOKING FOR LEECHES

Spray Can was at my house just after supper that night. We walked down by the canal with a flashlight to look at the leeches. You could see 'em too, big ones moving in the murk. Leeches are like nothing you've ever seen. Sometimes they're all sucked in tight and look like the top of a mushroom, and other times they're all stretched out and you think you're watchin' a slow water snake. We sat on a tree branch that hangs over the water and shined the light into the canal watching the water boogers, as Taco Bell would call them, 'cause they look like something that comes out of your nose when you sneeze.

"There's one," Spray Can said, pointing the light just below our feet. "Look how slow he moves."

"Yeah," I said. "He's got no place to go."

Spray Can left the light on him for a time, then

let it search around in the smelly water for another leech.

"I didn't give up today," he said after thinking about it for a bit. "I get into something, you know, I wanna see it through . . . beginning to end. My thumb just hurt bad, that's all."

"Is that what you were trying to prove when you came back?" I asked him. "That you could play with a hurt thumb?"

"Maybe at first," he said. "But then I started thinkin' about Ray."

Spray Can looked at me then.

"Ray don't come to my games. I thought about that. And I thought, What if he was here? What if he was standin' over on the sidelines with the rest of the parents? What if he got up early to drive me, to say thtuff like 'Have a good game'? You know, football thtuff. That's what I was thinkin' about. I wanted him to see how I was playin'. Maybe I was tryin' to prove somethin' to him, even though he wasn't there."

Spray Can's flashlight found another leech, stretched out but pullin' itself together into a ball.

"Is that what you think about?" Spray Can asked me.

"No," I said, reaching into the water and scooping up the leech.

"Well, what do you think about?" Spray Can asked.

"I don't know," I said, letting the leech attach itself to the back of my hand and try to break the skin, suck some of my blood. "I guess, I guess I think about losing. I don't want to lose."

We were both quiet for a moment, watching the leech.

"I get tired of people taking things away from me," I said.

"Least you had it to start with," Spray Can said. "Ray . . . he's always been gone."

"We don't got much between us, do we?" I said.

"We should get us some dogs, that's what Heat's done."

I pulled the leech off my hand and threw it into the water. We sat quiet for a moment, watching the leech slowly sink through the murk. Then Spray Can shined the light under his chin and made a scary face. It made me laugh. I guess it was his way of cheerin' me up. It made me sorry I had picked on him the way I had during the game. But I didn't tell him that. I couldn't. Not yet anyway.

THE PRICE OF WINNING

Everybody knows your name when you win a game. Somethin' happens. It's like you were sitting in the back of the class all year and one day the teacher puts you up front where everybody can see you. My English teacher, Miss Krone, said it has something to do with stardom.

"Everybody likes a winner," she said.

"Well, we've only won two games," I said.

"That's all it takes," she answered. "Stardom can be funny that way."

Stardom can also be funny in who it picks. Sometimes it's the last person you'd expect. Somehow, Taco Bell got all of the spotlight. Maybe because he was bigger than the rest of us. He ate up all the attention the way he would a whole watermelon. After the first win, we never saw Taco Bell again without someone talking to him about the great game he had, as if he'd done it all by himself. And the girls, that was the worst part. None of us had quite figured out girls yet. So when they started talking to us before we were ready for it, we didn't know why. Why were they all the sudden interested in us? No one was ever interested in what we were doing. It was strange having girls notice you overnight like you won the lottery or something. I'm not saying they all did, just a few. Katie Crofts was one, and she had a friend from Switzerland, a foreign-exchange student named Leisl, living at her house for a few months. They were the two most interested. I didn't think much of it, but soon as Taco Bell discovered it, he started acting like Elvis.

Taco Bell's not real smart, and he's kinda slow to change. But once he catches on, there's no stopping him. First he wore a clean shirt to school, you know, just to try it out. It was after he caught Katie looking at him, staring really; she'd had to stare to make sure he knew she liked him. The very next day he wears a shirt with no food stains or mud marks and Katie asks him to help her with her science. Next thing we know Taco Bell is struttin' through the halls with his hair combed and singing "Jailhouse Rock." He even started washing his face before comin' to school.

I guess girls will do that to you. It's just that, well, Taco Bell never seemed the lovestruck type. He's more the doughnutstruck type. He'll do anything for a doughnut. Once we were riding our bikes out behind the pastures and there was a dead cow. It was all bloated and covered with flies.

"I'll give you four doughnuts if you go sit on that cow," I said. I was only joking him. I didn't think he'd do it. But he did. He walked right up and sat back on that smelly carcass like it was his living-room couch. He sat there long enough for the flies to cover him too. Then he stood up, brushed him-self off, and said, "Let's go have a doughnut."

I thought about that when I saw him sitting at the same library table with Katie. She was sitting right next to him. I looked at him and thought maybe someone offered him a doughnut to sit by her. I imagined flies all over his face and then him saying something like "All right, pay up." But he never did. He just sat there, looking at those draw-ings of dissected frogs and laughing when Katie made faces.

Leisl was different. She didn't speak very good English, and she didn't really act like the other girls. She didn't giggle or pass notes or play with her hair. She also didn't know anything about football. So I was surprised when she came to football practice with Katie. They sat over in the shade under that big elm tree where Coach had asked us if we wanted to trade places with the band at the begin-ning of the season. It seemed strange to me. If they had heard that speech, they never would've come

back. But there they were, sitting like they were
waiting for some great thing to happen. It never
did. We ran our drills, learned new plays, scrimmaged. But they were there, every night. And
every night we said a few words to them, waved,
and walked home like we always do. Taco Bell
always stayed a little longer and talked to Katie.
Then he'd run to catch up with us about the time
we got to the canal. And he always had this big grin
on his face that made us want to throw him in with
the leeches. Finally, one day, we decided to test his
devotion.

"Hey, Taco Bell," Bam said. "We've all been
talkin' it over and, well . . . *bam!* . . . I don't know
what to say."

"What?" said Taco Bell.

"Here's what's up," I said. "We have a deal for
you. Each of us will give you one doughnut every
day until Christmas . . . that's four doughnuts a
day . . ."

"If?" asked Taco Bell, his eyes as big as cinna-
mon rolls.

"If you never say another word to Katie," I
finished.

I've never seen Taco Bell so confused. He paced
back and forth, holding his face and kicking gravel
into the canal. The rest of us stood there, holding
our mouths and trying desperately not to laugh.
Taco Bell was in agony. "Yes . . . no . . . yes . . . no,"

he kept saying, looking at his hands as if they had the answer.

"On weekends too?" he asked. "You'll give me doughnuts on weekends too?"

"If that's what it takes," Bam answered.

Taco Bell groaned. Then a sad look came over his face and he sat down on the bank and stared at the murky water.

"Looks like he's made his decision," Bam said. "Told you it wouldn't take long."

Taco Bell looked up at us then. "I guess," he said in a quiet voice. "I guess I'll have to go without doughnuts for a while."

We were all speechless. Taco Bell was in love.

ALL FOR ONE

All love aside, we had a job to do. We had to mark the end zones and we had to do it right. We had to call on as much power from nature as we could muster. We were playing Cyprus on Saturday. Undefeated Cyprus. We needed far more magic than four bladders could hold.

We called a team meeting.

Just after the sun went down, they started to show up. It was Friday night. We'd had a light practice that day, run through some plays with a dummy defense, then gone home to eat dinner and think about the game the next day. Bam passed the word at practice and they were there, all seventeen players standing under the elm tree wearing their "Prove it!" shirts. Bam addressed us first.

"We got a game tomorrow," he said. Then he was

quiet for a long time. "We got a game with a team we have never beat. They got that halfback, Conrad. Loves to run the ball . . . *bam*, like that. Loves to score touchdowns then toss the ball to one of us. Last year he scored, then jogged down the sideline and handed the ball to our coach. Remember that? *Bam!* I do. I remember every time we've ever lost. I don't need any more of those memories."

Bam looked around then, at all of our faces. He looked in our eyes.

"I won't take nothin' short of a win tomorrow," he said quietly but with a strained voice. "I won't. I show up tomorrow, it's to win. *Bam!* Heat has somethin' to say."

Bam sat down and put his hands on his head as if he was trying to keep himself down. Heat stood up slowly. I could tell he had thought about his speech all evening. I could tell he wanted to talk about the forces of nature, about primitive rituals, about the way one dog will challenge another, about marking your territory and sticking to it, fighting for it. But he didn't.

"Dogs will mark what's theirs and fight to the death over it," is all he said. Then he looked to me as if I was supposed to help him.

"That's why we're here," I said. "To lay claim to what's ours, to mark our territory so those boys from Cyprus know they got a fight comin'."

"How do we mark it?" one of the lineman asked.

"Same way the dogs do," I said. "We pee on whatever's ours." I looked everyone in the eyes then. Some laughed, but it was stomped out by the seriousness of the meeting.

"Pee?" the lineman said.

"It works for dogs," Heat said. "It works for all animals. It's a force of nature."

And with that, all seventeen of us made our way across the practice field and onto the game field, the field that was used only on Saturdays. We made a circle in the end zone, crossed swords for half the load, then ran to the other end zone trying not to mark our jeans before laying claim to the other half of the field. It was glorious standing there with all my teammates, calling on the forces of nature, looking up at a star-filled sky that would soon give way to the sun and the sounds of football. It was like we were preparing for battle, each of us counting on the other, yet alone in his thoughts, listening to his own heartbeat.

That was the closest we ever felt as a football team. We had never really felt a part of anything else. For years we had been together because we were losers. For years we had been the Titans that couldn't win a game. We were together because that's all we had. We couldn't do anything else; they wouldn't let us. If we tried baseball or basketball they'd say, "Oh, you're on that team that can't win a football game. You sure you want to play basketball?" I guess people make up their mind who you should be and they won't let you be anything else. The only one who can change it is you.

So when we took the field the next day against Cyprus, we were looking for some change. Cyprus had beat us every year for three years in a row. All they had to do was give the ball to Conrad and he'd score. Then he'd thank each of us as he made his way back to the huddle for the extra-point try.

"Thank you, thank you," he'd say. Then he'd score again. When I told Spray Can about Conrad, he got wild eyed. There's nothing Spray Can hates worse than a poor winner. All during warm-ups I'd sneak up behind Spray Can and whisper in his ear hole. "Thank you," I'd say, and Spray Can would go crazy.

By the time we kicked off to start the game, Spray Can was like a wild animal in a football suit. He made a beeline for Conrad, who was waiting for the ball to fall out of the air. I only remember two Cyprus guys who tried to block Spray Can; he plowed through them like a rocket blasting through a stand of trees. *Boom! Boom!* The others stepped out of the way. By the time Conrad saw Spray Can, it was too late. He didn't even have time to fake. Spray Can hit him like a freight train. *Boom!* The ball popped loose, and Spray Can rode Conrad all the way to the ground while the ball tumbled out of bounds. Then Spray Can smiled into Conrad's face mask. "Thank you," he said while Conrad groaned.

It was a long time before Conrad got to his feet.

In three plays, Cyprus would have to punt. It was the first time they had ever punted against us. We got the ball at about midfield and it took us six plays to score. We didn't pass, we didn't even run the sweep. "Let's beat 'em where they're strongest," Coach said. So we ran right at 'em. Nothing but power football. Me and Heat traded carries up the middle. Eight yards, six yards, eleven yards a carry. Finally I broke one loose for eighteen yards and it took Heat the next two carries to punch it into the end zone. We were only seven minutes into the first half and already we were ahead by a touch-down. Everybody on the sidelines started howling like dogs.

But the game wasn't over yet. Somehow Cyprus got it together enough to keep us out of their end zone for the rest of the half. Their offense threw everything they had at us, but our defense held. So when we sat in the shade for halftime, the score was still seven to nothin'. Coach had little to say.

"This is the time," he started. "This is the time to prove it. It's never over. You weren't done last week when you won. You're not done now. You got to go back out there to prove to yourselves one more time that you are winners."

Then he asked each one of us. "Are you a winner?"

"Yes!"

"Prove it!"

"Bam?"

"Yes!"

"Prove it!"

"Wing?"

"Yes!"

"Prove it! Prove it right now!"

He asked every one of us. And we all answered. Then he stopped, and for a long time he looked over at the other team across the field, sitting in their own spot of shade.

"What do you think they're thinking?" he asked us. "What do you think they're planning to do?"

He let us think about that for a moment.

"Do they want this game more than you do?" he asked.

"No!" we shouted.

"Do we want this game?"

"Yes!" we shouted.

"Then let's go prove it."

We ran back to the sidelines and waited for the kickoff to start the second half. As I lined up on the field, I could hear my heart pounding. I knew then that I was going to get the ball.

It was a line-drive kick that I had to scramble to pick up. It put me out of position, away from my wall of blockers. I didn't have much of a chance, but got what I could. I spun off the first few tacklers, but the third hit me so hard I thought I'd lost all my insides.

"Thank you," he said.

So, word had spread. I popped up quick, even though I wasn't breathing. Then I handed him the ball. I knew it was going to be a long second half.

Up until the last three minutes it was nothing but a defensive game. Then Cyprus started moving the ball. They gained two first downs and were past midfield for the first time all game. Conrad was back. They pitched the ball to him in what could've been the darkest moment of the game. He swung right, but instead of turning the corner, he stopped, set up, and threw the ball deep. We all froze and watched the ball spiral toward a tall split end who was running all alone for the end zone. The ball floated out ahead of him, it seemed to be waiting for him, hanging there in the air. . . . The split end was fast. In just a few long strides he made up the space between where he was and where the ball was going. He dove to make up the last few feet, arms outstretched, the end zone beneath him like a deep green pool. Waiting for that pass to drop was one of the longest moments in football history. The ball fell out of the sky and into the fingertips of the tall split end. His hands seemed enormous. He caught it. No, he dropped it! He couldn't hang on, and the ball slipped through his fingers and bounced out of the end zone while the split end belly-flopped onto the turf, mashed his face mask right into the ground where the night before we had all formed a circle, called on the forces of nature, and marked our territory.

He lay there on his stomach for a moment, clearing the grass from his face mask. Then he shook his helmet.

"Oooh, yuk, this stinks!" he cried.

It was a cry that rallied our defense, gave them the extra strength to hold their ground for the next three plays. Second down and two yards to go, and the defense walled up at the twenty yard line. Nothing, not an inch. They stood their ground, howling and barking and growling. On the last play of the series, Cyprus pulled up to pass again. But Spray Can blitzed, and before the quarterback could even set up, he was smothered by the stocky son of a mechanic.

With thirty seconds left in the game and our offense taking possession, Bam had only to bury the ball after one play. He went down on one knee, and while the clock ran out we all stormed the field. It was the first time Cyprus had lost to Olympus for as long as anyone could remember. It was also the first time that season I didn't look for my father on the sidelines. Suddenly it felt as if the whole world had changed somehow.

16

WHAT LOVE WILL
DO TO YOU

No one wants to do much on Saturday after you've lost a game. But when we started winning, all that changed. We hung out at the field longer, took our time getting home. And after we had showered, we ended up meeting at Spray Can's, 'cause Ray had a pop machine that cost only a dime. Sometimes Ray was there, under one of the cars. Hours would pass by and all we'd see of him was his feet. But mostly he was gone, chasing down a part somewhere or fishin' the Weber River by himself. When it got too cold to fish, Ray would sit by himself, tying flies. No one said anything to him, and he didn't say much to us. Only to Spray Can. And when he talked to his son, he never even looked at him, just gave him some order or reminded him of a chore that wasn't finished. And if we were there, we always helped Spray Can get the work done.

So after we beat Cyprus, we were all at Spray Can's. Ray was gone and we sat on this old couch out behind the shop, drinking pops, throwing the cans like footballs, and burping so loud our throats hurt. Taco Bell could get off the loudest burp. It sounded like a bear growling in the woods.

"Wait, wait, wait," he'd say, holding his arms out like he was conducting an orchestra. Then he'd open his mouth wide, expand his chest, and let it go.

"*Brrrrrrrrrrrrrrrrpf.*"

"Too bad Katie isn't here to hear that one," Bam said.

We all laughed, except for Taco Bell. He just looked at us and didn't say anything.

"C'mon," Bam said. "I'm jokin' you, man."

Taco Bell smiled.

"I mean," Bam continued. "Katie could probably beat it."

Then Bam burped himself.

"Like that," he said. "She could probably burp at least that loud."

That's all it took. Taco Bell charged like an angry bull and tipped the whole couch over. We were all laughing as he threw us around and hit us with the cushions.

"No one makes fun of my girlfriend!" he shouted.

Suddenly we were all quiet.

"Girlfriend?" we all said at the same time.

Taco Bell held a cushion in front of him. "Yes," he said. "She's my girlfriend."

"How can she be your girlfriend?" Heat asked. "Did she say so?"

"Yes, she did," Taco Bell said, hugging the cushion.

Then Bam asked the question we were all thinking but just couldn't find a way to say. It was a question we had wondered about since we first started winning; it was something we would wonder about until it happened to each of us.

"Did you kiss her?"

There was a long silence. We wanted to know everything. How to do it. What gum to chew. Did you have to do it more than once? Would a girl make fun of you if you didn't want to? Did it mean you would have to marry her? And most of all, what did it taste like? We waited for Taco Bell to answer, to answer everything we wanted to know about kissing in this one question.

"Did you kiss her?" Bam repeated.

"No," Taco Bell said quietly.

We were all relieved. Higher knowledge was put off until a later time, perhaps a time when we would be ready to accept its consequences. After all, kissing a girl would have to mean that you liked her, that you wanted to spend time talking to her instead of burping with your buddies. That was just too much to give up right then.

"So how can you say she's your girlfriend if you haven't kissed her?" I asked Taco Bell.

"'Cause she said she wants to be," he answered.

"You will have to kiss her, you know," I said as if it were a threat.

Taco Bell got this look on his face like he wanted to say "I will not." But he couldn't say it. Even he knew the inevitable, that yes, he would have to someday kiss a girl. I think secretly he was looking forward to it. But it would have to wait until after our last game.

THE CRAZY MAN

On Monday we ate in peace again. Taco Bell was the center of attention, sitting at the head of the table, talking about his sideburns, wishing they were longer. The more we won, the more he became like Elvis. I was happy to let him have the spotlight. I didn't feel much like talking to anybody anymore. All I wanted to do was play football. Everything else seemed like a waste of time. So I sat there quietly, eating my lunch and looking away from our table. That's when I saw Ed. I don't know how long he'd been staring at me, but it must've been for a long time. When I caught his eye, he mouthed the words "You're dead," and held up his fist. I wasn't in the mood for his threats, so I smiled at him and tossed a handful of cooked peas at him.

He went berserk.

He picked up all the peas and held them up to the faces of everyone at his table.

"I'll kill him!" he kept shouting. "I'm gonna kill him!"

When he had all his buddies as mad as he was, he stormed over to our table, kicking over chairs as he came. When he arrived, I stood up, shoved my lunch tray out of the way, and stared back at him. They all surrounded me. Taco Bell stopped singing, and for the second time that year, everybody in the whole lunchroom went quiet. Ed was so mad, he was having a hard time finding the right cuss words; so I started the conversation.

"Lose another game, Ed?"

This question, and I guess my willingness to ask it, caught Ed completely off guard. Ed's not real bright anyway. He likes people to back down when he tells them to. It confuses him when they don't. Ed fumbled around his head for the right answer, and all that he could come up with was: "So?"

He shouted, the way he shouts everything, to give it meaning. Before I could say anything else, and before Ed exploded with rage, the janitor stepped up from behind him.

"Yeah," he whispered. "I heard you guys lost again."

"Who are you!" Ed screamed before turning

around. When he did, he realized what he had done.

"Oh, nobody," the janitor calmly said. "Just the guy who can throw you out of here. Be too bad. You can't play football if you get kicked out of school."

"He threw these at me," Ed pleaded, holding up a pea.

"Oooh, that could be dangerous," the janitor said. "Too bad I didn't see it." And with that, the janitor turned back to his mop.

"When football is over," Ed sneered into my face. "So is your life!"

Ed and his buddies walked away like they were going off to prepare for war.

"You are crazy!" Taco Bell said.

"Yeah," I said. "Maybe I am."

"You're gonna get us all killed," Taco Bell said.

"You're not sittin' in the garbage dump any-more, are you?" I said back to him. "You wanna spend the rest of your life in someone else's crap, go ahead."

Taco Bell was quiet then. I think I hurt his feelings a little. But I didn't care. I wasn't gonna put up with it anymore.

"You do have something to prove, don't you?" Bam said, smiling. "It's about time."

Everybody laughed then, except me. I walked away and stood at a window and watched the cars drive by in the distance. I know it sounds strange, but I wished my father was there to see what had just happened in the lunchroom. I wished we could talk about it the way we talked about football. "Did you see me throw those peas?" I would ask him. "I don't know why I did it."

"You stood up to him," my father would say. "That's good, but be careful."

"Yeah, sure," I mumbled into the glass.

"Who are you talking to?" I heard someone say.

I was embarrassed, you know, how you would be if someone caught you talking to yourself. So I didn't turn around very fast.

"Nobody," I said still looking out the window.

"Oh. I thought maybe you were talking to me," I heard the voice say.

I turned around then and there she was, Leisl. I hate it when girls sneak up on you like that.

"I was just throwing some peas in there, and well . . ." It was the only thing I could think of to say, and it must've sounded pretty stupid.

"Peas?" she said. Now she was really confused. First I'm talking to the window; then I tell her about peas.

"Well, there's this guy in there, Ed. Fat Ed and I play football . . ."

"Football, I know," she said. "I've watched you in the big hard hat." She kind of giggled then.

"That's a helmet," I said. "You must think it's a stupid game."

I started to walk away then, but when I turned around she said, "I like football."

"Who are you talking to?" I said, acting surprised.

She laughed and walked toward me. "I would like you to tell me more about football."

"Okay," I said.

That day, after school, she walked home with me. I usually walk with Bam, so I had to hide until he gave up on me and went home alone. Then me and Leisl walked the long way, away from the canal and down past the small market. We stopped there for a soda and sat on the curb. Practice didn't start for another hour, so we had time to talk. I found some bottle caps and tried the best I could to explain football to her. It's funny, I never really thought about it. You know, why there is football, why I play. I lined up bottle caps for offense and defense and explained that one team was trying to put the ball in the other team's end zone.

"It's kind of like war," I said, maybe trying to understand it myself. "Each team has its own territory. They guard it for a while, then try and take ground from the other team. Whoever gets in the other team's territory the most, wins."

Leisl nodded her head.

"Let me introduce the players to you," I said.

Then I swept the bottle caps away so I could line them up as they came out.

"And now," I said in my announcer's voice, "playing left end and weighing ninety-eight pounds, The Flame."

I moved the bottle cap out to the left and Leisl laughed.

"At left offensive tackle, weighing a massive one hundred forty-two pounds, we have Rhino!"

I made cheering noises and Leisl clapped. Then I introduced the rest of the players. The Grizz playing left guard, Cobra at center, Taco Bell at right guard, Junior at right tackle, Rocket at wide receiver, Bam at quarterback, Heat at fullback, Lights at flanker, and, last but not least, Wing at halfback.

Leisl cheered. I started laughing. She had purple lips from drinking a grape soda. My lips turned orange. We were pointing at each other and laughing. Then she reached out and touched my lips, first to see if it rubbed off. Then she traced my smile.

"You're laughing," she said.

"Yes," I said.

"I've never seen you laugh."

"You've been watching me?" I asked her.

"Some," she said. "Mostly your face is long, like this."

She made a scowling face then, a face that I

didn't realize I was wearing until she pointed it out to me.

"My face looks like that?" I asked her.

"Yes," she said.

"No wonder everyone thinks I'm crazy."

"Your friend says you're angry," she said.

"Taco Bell?"

"Yes."

"Does everybody talk about me?"

"Some," she said. "Whenever they talk about football."

"I didn't think anybody else in the school cared about our games."

"They do," she said. "And they say that you are making the team win."

"Because I'm angry?"

Leisl didn't answer. She smiled at me and said, "You're not angry now."

I shook my head.

"Tell me more about football," she said, looking down at the bottle caps.

"I can't," I said. "I got practice tonight."

She looked disappointed. Then she reached down and picked up the halfback bottle cap, the one that was supposed to be me.

"Okay," she said. "You can tell me later?"

"Sure," I said.

We stood up and got ready to leave.

"Thanks for the soda," she said, rubbing her purple lips.

I laughed and rubbed my orange lips. "See you tomorrow," I said.

I walked home then, rubbing my lip for a while. But the closer I got to home, the longer my face got. By the time I got to practice, I was the angry one again.

UNCHARTED TERRITORY

That afternoon's practice went by quickly. We didn't learn any new plays for our game against Granite. We just worked on our sweeps and passes. Granite was big, but they were slow. Coach figured we could outrun them to the corners or deep on the pass. So mostly we worked on timing. It was a good practice, and we felt pretty confident about the Granite game. Granite had only one win so far that year; we all figured we could beat them. But we had one problem. It was an away game, across town. How were we going to get down there the night before to mark our territory? We sat down under the elm tree and tried to figure it out.

"I'm not walkin' all the way down there," Taco Bell said. "We wouldn't even be back by morning."

"We could sleep there," Bam offered. "Be like camping out."

"We wouldn't get enough sleep," I said. "We want to play well, don't we?"

We all agreed. The last thing we wanted to do was wake up tired. Besides, our parents would find out somehow and that would ruin everything. We had to find a way.

"Have your brother drive us," Heat said to Bam.

"Thought of that," Bam said. "They have their own pregame ritual. Every Friday night they all get together and have pizza; then they go down to Mortensen's junkyard and break things and yell and stuff. He's not gonna miss that to watch us all take a leak."

"Yeah," Taco Bell said. "Can't you see us asking him. 'Uh, Darrel, will you take our whole team to the bathroom, please?' "

Everybody laughed.

"I'm just gonna walk it," Heat said.

"Why don't I just get one of Ray's cars?" Spray Can offered.

"You drive?" Taco Bell said.

"Sure," Spray Can said. "I do it all the time. I'm almost sixteen."

"You're only thirteen," Bam said.

"I got a Idaho driver's license," Spray Can said. "Ray made me get it before we moved down here so I could help him get parts. You can drive when you're fourteen in Idaho."

"This is Utah," Bam said.

"You're fourteen?" Taco Bell said, realizing that Spray Can must have been held back a grade.

Spray Can looked down then. I guess he was embarrassed. We all knew he wasn't too bright, but none of us knew he'd had to repeat a grade.

"So I done fourth grade twithe," he said, wiping his face afterward. "Big deal. Are we goin' or not?"

"I'm in," I said, and stepped next to Spray Can.

"You're always in," Taco Bell said. "You're crazy."

I just nodded my head.

"I could use a little road trip," Bam said, stepping next to me.

It didn't take long for everyone else to join in, everyone, that is, except Taco Bell. He just stood there looking down at his feet and kicking at a weed in the dry grass.

"Wonder what Katie will say when she finds out her boyfriend is a chicken?" I said.

For the second time that season, Taco Bell went crazy over a girl. He must've really been in love. He came at me with everything, swinging, kicking, screaming. He was like the Tasmanian Devil. It took everybody else to hold him down.

"I'll kill you!" he kept yelling. "I'll kill you!"

His face was red and he was breathing like an animal. He hit me only a couple of times, which didn't really hurt. But when Taco Bell settled down, Bam had a bloody nose.

"Why don't you hit like that in a game . . . *bam*, just like that, *bam, bam!* Bring that girl to the game and we'll make fun of her to rile you up."

Everybody laughed, even Taco Bell. But it took him a little longer.

"I woulda gone, you guys," he said. "You don't have to say stuff like that."

"You're the crazy one," I said. "You shoulda seen your face."

Taco Bell laughed. "Well, you looked pretty scared."

"Yeah," I said. "I guess I was."

Taco Bell looked at me then, wanting to tell me that he wasn't mad anymore, that there was no reason to be scared. He didn't understand that it wasn't him I was afraid of. I didn't even know for sure what it was. I couldn't explain how I felt. But Spray Can knew. He'd been alone long enough to know how it felt. And he knew I didn't want to talk about it.

"Ray goes for parts most weekends," Spray Can cut in. "There's always a few cars around with keys in 'em."

"So we meet at the garage on Friday night," I said, nodding at Spray Can.

"That'll work," Heat said.

That's how it was settled. We would mark our territory on someone else's field. It would be the true test of the force of nature.

ON THE ROAD

We couldn't think of anything else the rest of the week. We even had a hard time concentrating at practice.

"Go home and meditate," Coach said to us. "Think about the spoils of victory. A loose mind will spell defeat, for all of us. Meditate, men. Meditate on the victory at Marathon, the conquest of the Gauls. Meditate."

And with that, he closed his eyes and waved us home from the last practice before Saturday's game.

It was Friday afternoon. D day, Taco Bell called it. "The day we drive."

We spent the rest of the afternoon at the canal, sitting on the wooden bridge tossing pebbles into the water. No one said much; we just stared at the tiny splashes until they turned orange from the set-ting sun. Then we looked at each other as serious as we could.

"This is it," Bam said. "See you in a couple hours."

We all went home to dinner, to sit nervously until it was dark enough to leave.

"I'm going with Taco Bell," I told my mom.

"To do homework, I hope," she said.

I didn't answer. And I didn't look back.

I was the first to arrive at Spray Can's that night. Spray Can was right. Ray was gone for the weekend. At least this time he'd left Spray Can with some food. He had eaten two TV dinners by the time I had gotten there. He cleared the empty trays off the couch for me and I sat down with his dog Bob. There was a space movie on and Spray Can was cheering for the bad guy, of course.

"Fry his butt with the laser," he shouted at the TV. "Toast him!"

Then he looked at me.

"You can get something from the fridge if you want," he said.

I rummaged around and found half a candy bar. I broke a piece off and gave it to Bob. Then I sat down and looked at Spray Can.

"Do you think I'm crazy?" I asked him.

"Sure," Spray Can said. "Who isn't?"

He laughed then for a moment before looking back to the TV.

"Toast him!" I shouted.

Just then the bad guy in the black space suit blew up from a direct laser hit.

"Oooh," we groaned.

"Fried from the inside out," Spray Can said. "What a way to go."

We heard a knock on the window. When I turned around, I could see Bam and Heat looking through the dirty glass. Spray Can opened the garage door out front, and even though it was a cold night, he left it open and turned on the heater. It wasn't long before everyone else was there. Except for Taco Bell.

"I knew we should've gone by his house," Bam said.

"He'll be here," I said. "We got time."

Heat's dogs were a little nervous around Bob. It always took Bob a bit to warm up to the four Labs. Bob followed them everywhere they went, and it was funny seeing him try to keep up with all four. He was like a mother hen trying to keep four young roosters out of trouble. Heat's dogs didn't help much; they were into everything, their big tails swinging back and forth and knocking all kinds of stuff over. Spray Can moved the TV into the garage and everybody found something to sit on; some empty can or box or broken chair. The space show ended and a Western was on. We were cheering for the Indians when Taco Bell finally showed up. His face had blue stuff all over it and his hands were sticky. But his eyes were all excited.

"There's a wedding on at the church behind Smoky Joe's," he said as if it were better than Christmas.

"So?" Bam said.

"So . . ." Taco Bell said. "There's lots of food and they got it all set up in the back, you know, close enough to that hole in the fence to make out with all kinds of cake and those chocolate things. . . . It's good."

"We got a mission tonight," Heat said seriously.

"We can't do it on an empty stomach," Taco Bell said. "Let's eat first, then go. Besides, I can't go yet anyway; I just went an hour ago."

Sparky slugged him.

"You bozo," he said. "I been holdin' it all night."

"I'm gonna pee my pants if we don't get goin' now," Flame said.

"C'mon," Taco Bell pleaded. "We gotta do more than pee tonight. We got us a car, right?"

We all looked at Spray Can then.

"Do we?" I asked him.

Spray Can was quiet for a long time. He wanted the suspense to build.

"Do we have a car?" Flame asked. "Huh?"

Spray Can smiled. "We do," he said. "A very sthpecial car. Follow me."

No one dared say a word. We followed Spray Can as if he were some fairy godfather about to deliver on a dream. He walked straight out through the open garage door, around the corner of the small brick building, and stood beside the most amazing car any of us had ever seen. A 1957 Bel-Aire convertible. It had long fins. It was blue and white. It had no roof. It had a radio. And Spray Can had the keys.

"Gentlemen," Spray Can said like a royal butler, "your car awaits."

We all jumped on him, rubbing his head and calling him the greatest player of all time.

"This is one for the Titan Hall of fame," Taco Bell yelled as we all climbed in.

It wasn't easy getting seventeen guys in that car. We had to squeeze four in the front, seven in the back, and six in the trunk. The little guys were voted in the trunk, including Sparky. But they didn't care. This would be one of the greatest adventures of our lives; they'd take it however they could get it. When we were all in, and Spray Can had the engine running, Heat tried to call his dogs.

"No," we all shouted. "There isn't enough room."

"But they've always been there," Heat said. "It's theirs too."

"Sorry," we all said. "We'll have to do it without them this time."

And with that we drove away, into our dreams. We had crossed that invisible point of no return. We were suddenly teenagers cruisin' in a convertible and so full of reckless adventure, we could've driven beyond the horizon to conquer worlds unknown, maybe even danced with girls. We were that sure of ourselves.

The first stop, of course, was Smoky Joe's. Everybody called him Smoky Joe because he smoked cigars all the time. There was always a cloud of smoke around his head. We parked across the street and got out quietly. Smoky Joe was old, so we knew he'd be asleep already. We crept along the side of his house, always staying low and in the shadows. We crossed under the wire clothesline in his backyard to the hole in his fence. It was a shortcut we often took, especially if we were being chased by Fat Ed. The hole was small and Ed always had a hard time squeezing through. If he ever got close, you were sure to lose him at Smoky Joe's. We lay down in the shadows. Then everybody looked at me.

"You're the crazy one, Wing," Bam said. "Go get us some food."

I moved to the hole in the fence and surveyed the grounds. Most of the people had gone home, but there were a few left up by the church. The food table stood off a bit, and no one was around it. There were bottles of soda in crates under the table and big chunks of cake on top. Trouble was, it was a good thirty-yard sprint from the hole in the fence to the table. And there was no cover, only a stretch of lawn.

"Would you like drinks too?" I said.

"Of course," Taco Bell said. "Bring those peach sodas."

With those instructions I jumped through the hole in the fence and shot straight for the table. I sprinted as fast as I could and slid under the table like I was sliding home. In less than three seconds I had a crate of pop and was headed back to the hole in the fence. The bottles rattled as I skidded to a stop.

"Enjoying the wedding?" I asked.

"Oh, very much," Bam said. "Have they cut the cake yet?"

"I believe they have," I said. "Would you like a piece?"

"That would be delightful," Bam crooned.

"Be right back," I said, running off toward the table.

Just as I slid in this time, a man in a white jacket turned around from the people he was talking to and walked to the food table. I crouched down under the table and waited. Another man in a white uniform walked up to him.

"Alex," the first man said. "I don't think we'll be serving more cake tonight. Why don't we clear this table and start cleaning up."

Then the man in the white jacket walked back to the people he was talking to and Alex was left to clear the cake himself. I heard him stacking dishes and I looked over at the hole in the fence for further instructions. Bam was there giving me hand signals. *Wait*, I could see him signal. *Wait. Wait. Wait. Now!*

I jumped up and looked first for Alex, second for the biggest slab of cake on the table. I found the one they had been cutting from and it was almost too big to carry. But I didn't have time to cut it. I grabbed the whole thing and took off running.

It would've been a clean getaway too, if I hadn't grabbed a part of the tablecloth with it. Dishes crashed to the ground behind me, Alex turned around, every wedding guest turned around. And there I stood, with this huge cake in my hands. There was only one thing to do: Run! I headed for the fence like it was the end zone. Alex was fast. In no time he was right behind me. When he didn't catch me instantly, he became even more intent on tackling me. I slipped his grasp just before I got to the hole in the fence, and I could tell he was going to give it one more effort. I dove through the hole just as he lunged for me. I heard him hit the ground as I sailed through the hole and landed right on top of Taco Bell. Somehow the cake survived the hand-off. Taco Bell was up quickly. He handed off to Bam, who turned and handed off to Heat. Spray Can was already in the car, and so was nearly everybody else. Just as I got to my feet, I heard Alex squeezing through the fence. I took off again as fast as I could go, but Alex was right behind me, running at full tilt.

"Start the car!" I yelled to Spray Can.

I heard the Bel-Aire fire to life just as I ran under the clothesline.

You know, Smoky Joe is a short man. So when he strung his clothesline, he hung the wires just *below* six feet. Which is too bad for Alex, because my guess is he stands just *above* six feet. I guess that because one of those wires caught him right under the nose. I didn't see much, but Bam said it looked like someone had thrown up a bag of white laundry.

"There were arms and legs everywhere." Bam said. "Then he landed with an awful groan. He got up pretty slow."

By the time Alex had figured out what hit him, we were on the road to another victory.

THE HARD WAY

There's nothing like a Friday night, lots of cake, and all the pop you can drink. Spray Can was a much better driver than we had figured. Turns out he drives all the time for Ray. He drives slow, though; says he doesn't want to draw any attention to himself. So we poked along the back roads all the way to Granite High School, where we would play the next day's game. We drank so much pop that by the time we got there we were so ready to pee that no one saw the guys sitting in the bleachers. We just ran onto the field, marked one end zone, and ran to do the other trying not to wet our pants. Then we met at midfield to talk about the game, the way we would if we were at home.

"Well, what do we have here?" we heard someone say. It startled us because we thought we were alone.

There was only seven or eight of them. But they were big; they were at least a year older than us. We'd find out later that they played on the team that would pound Ed Stebbing's team the next day. They stood there looking at us, trying to figure us out.

"You come down and piss on our field," one of 'em said, "you just might make someone angry."

"That's the idea," I said without thinking.

"Yeah?" the biggest one said, stepping up to my face.

Before I could say anything else, he threw a forearm that caught me in the head and knocked me to the ground. I've never been hit so hard, by anyone. Stars shot through my head. I couldn't hear anything. Before I could stand up, Bam landed on the ground next to me.

"You little boys got anything else to say?" the big one said to us.

No one said a thing. I stood up and he grabbed me by the shirt and threw me down. Then he turned and punched Taco Bell in the stomach. It may have been the only thing that saved us. Taco Bell threw up half a wedding cake and four bottles of peach soda. The boys from Granite laughed. They slapped our faces as we tried to walk away.

"Go on home, boys," they said. "Come back when you're big enough to play this game."

Then they shoved at us and kicked our butts as

we went by. We crossed the field in darkness, climbed into the Bel-Aire like battle-fatigued soldiers, and drove away.

None of us said a word on the way back. Except for Taco Bell.

"My stomach hurts," he kept saying.

When we got to Spray Can's, everybody just climbed out of the car and walked home. We didn't even look at each other. I guess everybody figured we deserved it for stealing cake from a wedding. It was our punishment and we tried to take it like men. But when we were around the corner, we could hear Spray Can kicking an empty gas can. *Bang!* You could hear him kick it, and it would rattle off the wall. *Bang!* I heard it nearly all the way home. Even when I knew I was too far away to really hear it, that can clanged around in my head, *bang!*

The next morning we were so out of it that Coach had to stop us in the middle of warm-ups to ask us what was wrong.

"Did you all spend the night dreamin' the season was over?" he shouted at us. "Did you just figure that you didn't want to make it to the play-offs?"

No one said anything.

"We win this game and we're on to the play-offs, fourth seed out of four teams. We lose and it's our last game. Has anybody here been to the play-offs?"

No one raised a hand.

"It's worse than I thought," he said.

We knew we were in trouble. We just didn't know how to get out of it. We were so demoralized by Friday night's pounding that no one wanted to ever play the game again. Lucky for us, Granite had their worst game of the year. Every time they got a drive going, they fumbled. Their offense was having all kinds of trouble. Their only score came late in the first half when they blocked one of our many punts and their big defensive tackle landed on the ball in the end zone. They didn't even make the extra point—another fumble. So when we broke for halftime, the score was only six to nothing for Granite.

"It oughta be a hundred to nothing the way you guys are playing," Coach said. "What is it going to take to pull you guys out of it? By some miracle we're still in this game. If we want to win, all we have to do is play football. I don't know what it is you guys are playing. It's not football, it's not the game you played last week against undefeated Cyprus. You knocked off the best team in the league, and now you're losing to the worst. Let's get it together. We're a better team than this. We're the Titans!"

It didn't inspire us much. Granite kept making their mistakes and we kept making ours. It was as if neither team wanted to win. Every time we made a mistake, I got madder and madder. I'd throw a block downfield that would send the linebacker sailing off the field like a bowling ball, but when I'd turn around Bam would be at the bottom of the pile, caught from behind before he could even hand the ball off.

Coach was helpless. No speech about victory, or about the Romans, or even General Patton, could pull us out of it. We punted with two minutes left and it looked like it was going to be the ball game. I grabbed Spray Can before he went out on defense. I could hear that *bang!* I could hear Spray Can kicking the gas can.

"Kick the can," I said to Spray Can.

"What?" he said back to me.

"Like you did last night," I said. "Kick the can like you did last night when you were mad. Kick the can!"

Spray Can looked at me as if a light went on. He ran out onto the field and stood right over the center on the first play, his hands moving nervously, his feet jumping. I knew he was going to blitz.

The quarterback barked the signal.

Spray Can pumped his arms.

The center hiked the ball.

Spray Can charged. He charged like a madman. *Bang!* He was through the line. *Bang!* He hit the quarterback. *Bang!* He punched the ball loose. The ball tumbled away, bouncing in slow motion. Spray Can threw the quarterback aside and dove on the ball. Our whole team erupted. Now it was our turn to score. With less than a minute to play, we remembered why we had put on our pads that morning.

But as our offense was taking the field, the older Granite team, the team that was about to hand Ed Stebbings his worst loss of the year, the team who only the night before had watched us desecrate their field and had made us pay for it, formed a line at the back of the end zone and started chanting like blood-crazed warriors.

"Defense! Defense! Defense!"

Our first three plays went nowhere. We were inside the thirty, but it was as if every word the older team chanted set up a barrier, a stone in a wall we could not push through. On third down, I had gone downfield to block. I caught sight of the players at the back of the end zone. I found the big guy that had slammed me to the ground the night before. He was shouting the loudest. He was enjoying seeing us crash and burn. I ran back to the huddle.

"Throw me the ball deep," I said to Bam. "A deep post. I can burn him."

"I'm not getting enough time!" Bam yelled back at me. "They're on me before I can even throw the ball."

"Then run the 38 pitch to Heat," I said. Then I turned to Heat. "But pull up and launch the ball to the back of the end zone. I'll be there."

"Do it!" Bam said.

I lined up wide in the backfield. Heat looked at me before Bam started the cadence. He could get it to me, I knew he could get it to me. I heard Bam bark: "Set! Hut! Hut!"

I started off inside to get around the linebacker, cut outside to get on the outside shoulder of the deep safety, then veered toward the middle of the field. I could hear the crashing of helmets behind me. And I could see the big guy at the back of the end zone, standing without his helmet on, egging his younger team on.

"*Defense!*" I heard him scream. I set my path right for him, then looked over my shoulder. Heat launched a high, arcing, wobbly spiral that looked like it was going to be too deep. I blew past the deep safety, running madly, looking over my shoulder, then at the big guy, the ball, the big guy. He saw me coming just as I reached out to haul the pass in only two steps before crashing out of the end zone. I didn't slow down. The big guy stepped to the side, but I stepped with him. *Bang!* We hit heads. Too bad I was the only one wearing a helmet. He went down hard and came up angry. I rolled past him and jumped up just as the referee signaled touchdown.

The big guy didn't know who hit him until I pulled off my helmet to celebrate. I've never seen anyone so mad. One of his buddies was trying to hand him a towel to wipe the blood from his nose. He threw it away and screamed at us.

"You haven't won yet, you lucky little creep!"

Then he marched around behind the end zone, throwing his arms up and trying desperately to motivate the younger team. But it was no use. Heat punched in the extra point and tossed the ball to the maniac just before the final gun went off. He threw it back at us and was so out of control his teammates had to drag him away. Titans 7, Granite 6.

"We won," I whispered to my father. But he couldn't hear me, he wasn't there. While everyone else was celebrating the victory, I walked away with my mother. She didn't say a word, just drove me to the hospital while the rest of the team pushed and shoved and congratulated each other. I watched them from the backseat of my mother's car, and I thought about them all the way to the hospital. That's where my father was then. He got to be too much for my mother to take care of. She had to work, she said. She had to put him someplace where someone could watch after him all the time.

"Why don't you just quit work?" I said.

She got angry then.

"Why don't you quit football?" She said. "Why don't you quit everything and stay here twenty-four hours a day yourself?"

I didn't answer. Truth is, I would've if I'd thought

that's what my father wanted me to do. But I knew how much he loved football. And every time I played, it made me angry that he wasn't there to see it. It made me so angry I was crazy, just as crazy as they all thought I was. Every time I threw a block, I threw it hard. I wanted to knock someone down for every time I looked over at the sidelines and didn't see my father. I wanted to change it all somehow, but I couldn't and it made me crazy mad sometimes. But at least we were winning. No one could believe it. It was going to be the greatest season ever, and I didn't care. All I wanted to do was make someone else hurt as much as me, as much as my father.

"We made the play-offs," I whispered to him. Then I waited for him to whisper something back through the tubes in his throat. But he didn't. I sat down on the floor beside his bed.

"You don't have to stay here tonight," I heard my mother whisper.

I opened my eyes a little and looked at her. I must have fallen asleep. It was dark in the room. She looked tired.

"I'm afraid," I said, coming out of the sleep and not knowing why I was even saying it. It was like I was in a dream and I was watching myself talk about things I didn't understand.

"It's okay," my mother said. "I'm a little afraid myself."

She sat down in a chair then and stared at me.

"You look like him, you know," she said to me. "In a few years you'll look just the way he did when we first met. I'd like to have that back right now. With nothing in between."

She closed her eyes and talked softly. "It hasn't been easy, I know. Not for you, not for any of us. . . . You should get some sleep."

Even as she said it, the very thought of it put her out like she'd been hypnotized to fall into a deep sleep whenever the word was mentioned. Within moments she was breathing long and heavy. Beside me the pump that filled my father's lungs breathed for him. The same rhythm, day and night, not slower when he slept, not faster when he was awake. Steady. My own breath fogged the steel bar of his bed. There we were, the three of us sharing the same air, living and dying with each breath, afraid to breathe, afraid not to.

21

HOW TO PLAY FOOTBALL

On Monday morning there was a huge banner stretched across the building. WAY TO GO, TEAM! it said, and all our names were on it. Taco Bell thought it was the greatest honor he could ever receive. I guess the only name he saw was his. He walked into the school like he'd just been crowned prince of the world. He was wearing his jersey so everyone would know who he was. Fact is, the only ones who really knew him were some of the guys in the band, and Katie. But Taco Bell walked through the hallways saying hi to everybody. And if there was a group of girls, he'd kinda saunter by, glance over at them, and raise his eyebrow like Elvis. When he did it to Katie, she said, "Oh, honey. Did you hurt your eye in the game?"

That's the kind of day it was. Even lunchtime was strange. We ate like kings, without looking over our shoulders. Ed and his pals were nowhere to be found. We knew they had lost, that Granite had beaten them up pretty badly. Somethng like 28 to 6. But, it wasn't like them to not show up. No one was complaining, but it was strange.

"Wonder where Fat Ed and his buddiesth are," Spray Can said.

"Who cares," Taco Bell said. He was too busy celebrating. After lunch he ate six ice-cream sandwiches. "Victory lunch," he called it, stuffing them into his mouth. The whole world seemed to revolve around us then. There was nothing in our way, nothing wrong with our universe, our world at school. Until I went back to my locker. That's when I figured out where Ed Stebbings had been during lunch. There was a note taped on my locker. YOU'RE STILL A LOSER, it said in red ink, Ed's trademark. And when I opened my locker I found that he had shoved the fire extinguisher hose through one of the little vents at the top and filled the whole thing up with water. Everything was soaked; all my books, my papers, my jacket. It meant that a week's worth of homework would have to be redone. I guess the big guy from Granite was so mad he took it out on Ed. In turn, Ed took it out on me. Funny how anger gets passed around like that.

"I'll make him pay for this," I said into my locker.

"Who are you talking to?" I heard Lcisl say.

"You're always sneaking up on me," I said to her, turning around.

"You're always talking to yourself," she said. Then she looked at the inside of my locker. "Why is everything wet?"

"It's a long story," I said. "Do you have any dry paper?"

She reached in her bag and found me a pad of paper. I pulled out my soggy books and we walked outside and spread them out to dry. It was a warm day for late October. Seemed it was the first time I had noticed the weather for a long time. I copied my wet assignments onto dry paper and tried to explain more football to Leisl. I set up leaves and sticks as the players, but when I went to place a rock for the halfback, Leisl moved it and set down the bottle cap.

"This is you, right?" She said.

I was surprised. "Yeah, that's me, the orange soda."

I went through all the power plays, the pitches and sweeps, and finally the pass plays. I explained the offense to her, what each player does on every play. I told her what makes a good guard, a good tackle, center, end, quarterback, fullback, and halfback.

"See, each is different," I said. "They each have something different to do. And they have to do it right or it won't work, no matter how good just one of them is."

Then I showed her what would happen if the guard pulled the wrong way, or if the quarterback handed off to the wrong man, or the center hiked it on the wrong count.

"Lots of things can go wrong," she said.

"Yeah," I said. "Lots can go wrong. That's what makes winning so great. There's just not much chance of it."

"Where did you learn it all?" she asked me.

"Mostly from my father," I said.

"You're father plays football too?"

"He did, a long time ago. He doesn't play anymore. He doesn't do much of anything anymore."

She smiled, I suppose she was thinking my father had just lost interest in the game, that he was like a lot of fathers, getting older and caring less about football.

"He— he's dying," I said.

I stood up to leave then, but I couldn't think of a place to go. It was like my mind went blank and I was lost. I just stood there, looking around, waiting for someone to point me in the right direction.

"You want to leave?" Leisl asked.

"I don't know," I said. "I don't know."

"Stay here," she said. "Just a little longer."

I sat down.

We didn't say much more for a long time. We just sat together. Somehow I believed she knew how I felt. Maybe it was because she had been away from her family for a while. Maybe she had felt lost too. I wanted to tell her about my father, about everything we had done together, about the way he could put his big hands around a football, or on my shoulders and make me feel like I was the only thing in his life. I wanted to tell her I was angry because I didn't have that anymore, I wasn't part of anybody's life anymore. I wanted to tell her that it wasn't fair, that none of it was fair. But I couldn't. And I didn't have to. She understood how I felt and she sat there with me so I wouldn't be alone. We watched the clouds for the rest of the afternoon. They were moving away from us, seemed like the whole world was moving away from us, slowly spinning off and leaving us stranded.

TACO BELL'S CRASH

"**F**our teams make the play-offs," Darrel explained to us. "They try to set it up so that number one and number two end up in the championship game. You guys are number four. That means you're supposed to be an easy win for the first-place team, so they can coast into the championship game. Two and three play at the same time you do. Most of the time two wins, so they play one for the championship. But you never know. A team like you guys can come into the play-offs with a lot of momentum and mess everything up, surprise everyone by kicking butt and taking the whole thing. That's what's so fun about the play-offs. Anyone can win."

We were on our way to Bud's Sporting Goods. Darrel was glad to drive his little brother anywhere then, long as it had something to do with football.

We were on our way to buy tape for Bam's ankle. I found out later that Bam never really had a sore ankle. He just had this Johnny Unitas trading card that he taped to his ankle every game for good luck. Bam was the most superstitious of all of us, and he wasn't about to change anything for the play-offs.

"Hey, Wing," Darrel said. "Can you pull off a win here in the first round?"

"Yeah," I said, not wanting to play Darrel's psychology games. He was always playing coach with us, trying to push us. It didn't sit well with me. It was like he was trying to be a part of something that wasn't his.

"I know you will," he said. "We just got to find a way to get you mad before the game." Then he laughed. He didn't understand. He'd known about my father all season and still he didn't understand. He thought it was only about winning. It wasn't. It was about not losing. It was about not wanting to lose anything anymore. But Darrel didn't understand that. He just hadn't lost enough in his life.

"Whatever," I said, looking out the window.

"You're a hard one to figure, Wing," he said.

"You just don't get it, do you?" I said angrily.

"I guess not," Darrel said.

We got Bam's tape, and when we got home, Darrel threw us the ball for a while before practice started. That's when we found out about Taco Bell. We were standing in the street when Katie rode her bike up and stopped beside us. She'd been crying, and she had this worried look on her face.

"Tyler's hurt," she said, calling Taco Bell by his real name. She was trying not to cry again. "He's really hurt."

"What happened?" Bam asked.

"He crashed his bike," she said. "Bad."

"Where is he now?" I asked her.

"He's home, but I think they're going to take him to the hospital."

Taco Bell didn't live too far from Bam. We could cut through a few yards, hop a couple fences, and we'd be there.

"We'll meet you there," I said to Katie as we jogged away.

I thought about Taco Bell's mom on the way over. She was always against football. Said it was too dangerous. Poor Taco Bell had to take piano lessons just to make her happy. She's big, like him; and she can make your life miserable if she doesn't like you. And she doesn't like Bam. She blamed her son's "football fascination," as she called it, on Bam.

"Your ancestors must've been barbarians," she said to him one time when he was waiting for Taco Bell to finish up a lesson.

"Yes, I think they were," Bam said, thinking she meant they cut hair. He was just trying to be polite. But ever since then, she hasn't liked him. And she's never liked football. She said Tyler would get hurt someday, it was only a matter of time. Well, I wanted to rush into his house and tell her he'd never been hurt playing football and that this was proof that football was safer than just about anything else he could be doing. I wanted to tell her that if he'd been playing football instead of riding his bike, he'd be fine, no injuries, no hospital, nothing.

When we got to Taco Bell's, Bam stopped on the porch and sat down.

"I'll wait here," he said.

I was about to knock on the door, but it opened. It was Taco Bell's mother and she was helping her banged-up son limp out the door to the car.

"Excuse us, please," she said.

Taco Bell wasn't wearing anything but his underwear. His whole left side was scraped and red. His mother had scrubbed the wounds and put some kind of salve on them, and they were shiny and raw.

Taco Bell whimpered. He was in so much pain, he didn't pay attention to us at all. I'm not sure he could see us anyway. The side of his face was scraped pretty bad and his eye was nearly swollen shut. He winced with every step.

"Is he gonna be all right?" I asked his mother.

"That's what we're going to find out," she said dramatically.

Then she loaded him carefully into the car. He

looked at us through the window, his eyes red and dry from crying too much. He didn't try to wave, or say good-bye. He just looked at us. It was strange because we didn't know what he was thinking.

"Guess he won't play the piano for a while," Bam said.

None of us laughed. We just stood there in the driveway, not knowing what else to say. Finally, Katie said what we were all thinking.

"What about football—do you think he'll be able to play?"

Bam didn't say anything. He looked at me for an answer.

"He'll play," I said, not really believing it myself. "He'll play."

THE BIG SCAB

Taco Bell didn't make it to a practice that whole week. He even stayed home from school the first two days, and his mother wouldn't let us even see him until Wednesday. When she finally let us in the house, Taco Bell was sitting at the piano, staring at a music book. When he saw us, he quickly moved to the couch and sat down. He looked like a villain in a Batman comic book. Half his body was a scab, the other half was perfectly normal. He was wearing shorts and a T-shirt, so we could see most of his scabs. They were the biggest scabs we had ever seen.

"Let's see you eat one of those," Bam said.

Taco Bell laughed. "My mom won't let me," he said.

"We brought you these," I said, handing him a

pack of doughnuts. "You can save the scabs for later."

"Doughnuts!" he said excitedly. Then he tore the end off the box and had one eaten before he even knew what kind they were.

"Are you going to make it to Saturday's game?" I asked him.

Just then his mother walked by.

"Thanks," he said looking sideways at his mother. "I could use some help with my homework."

When she was gone, he leaned forward and whispered to me.

"She won't let me out of the house."

"We gotta have you," I said. "We've been working Farts all this week but he's not getting it."

"Farts is too slow to pull," Taco Bell said.

"Tell me about it," Bam said. "He don't block much either. I'm gettin' killed in the scrimmages. You know what it'll be like in the game? *Bam!* . . . That's what it will be like."

"You gotta make it," I said. "It's the play-offs."

Taco Bell touched the scab on his cheekbone softly and gave us this worried look. Then his mother called him from the other room.

"Tyler," she said, "you need to finish practicing."

"I will," he answered.

"Find a way," I said. "Find a way."

When Bam and I left, neither one of us believed

Taco Bell would make it to another game that season. We went through our last practice on Friday pushing Farts as hard as we could, but he just wasn't getting it. He wasn't fast enough to pull for the lead block; instead he just got in the way. And when he blocked straight ahead, he couldn't move sideways fast enough to pick up the stunts the defense was throwing at him. He was slow and confused. But he had a lot of desire. We tried to get him up for it, tried to make him believe he could do it. But it was no use. He'd get all excited and shake like a true believer overcome with the spirit of football; then his feet would get all tangled up and he'd fall over on his can. He'd lie there, spit his mouthpiece out, and moan, "I can't do it, I just can't do it."

Poor Farts. He just didn't have it. We decided we'd have to run everything to the left side and hope that he could hold off his man long enough for us to get a play off. We would also have to score early, because once they figured out where the weak spot was, they'd pound it all day long.

That night, after we had piled into an old station wagon at Spray Can's and driven to the field to mark our territory, we stood at midfield and tried to figure out how to beat West. West was the first team we had played that season. They had beaten us badly. We were sure they were counting on an easy win. That was about our only advantage. That and the forces of nature. Nothing else seemed to be going right. First off, Ray finished the '57 Bel-Aire, so our cruiser was gone and we were stuck with this station wagon that was in for a muffler. Then when we got to the field, nobody could go. Me and Heat marked both end zones ourselves. Luckily his dogs were there or it would've been a pretty poor offering to the gods of nature.

That made me think. So we didn't have the cruiser. It hadn't been big enough to get us all in anyway, at least not including Heat's dogs. The wagon had enough room. It wasn't fancy, but it got the job done. Maybe our offense for the next day had to be the same way. So Farts was slow. That just meant he wasn't as fancy as Taco Bell. But Farts was big, bigger than Taco Bell. He ate more too, which gave him tremendous gas. That's why we called him Farts. So maybe we just had to figure out a way to get the job done without pulling; you know, just basic plug-up-the-hole blocking. We didn't need Farts downfield, or to pull around the corner on the sweeps. We just needed him to keep the defense out.

We set up the offensive line right there in the dark. Then I marked off Fart's territory.

"Nobody gets through this part of the field," I said to him. "All you have to do is keep people out."

"And we don't care how you do it," Bam added. "Just stop 'em, *bam!*, like that. Every play."

By the look in Fart's eyes, I could tell that a huge burden had been lifted from his shoulders. He didn't have to keep track of which direction he had to pull, or how to pass block, or who to pick up downfield. All he had to do was keep people out of the backfield.

"Hold your ground," Heat said. "That's all we want you to do."

When we got back to the station wagon, I looked at it proudly. "This will work," I said to myself. "This will work."

THE FIRST
PLAY-OFF GAME

was up early the next day. I had been getting up earlier on Saturdays ever since my father
went to the hospital. At first I did it because he
wasn't there to get my gear ready. But I think the
real reason I did it was to be alone with him again.
Even though he wasn't there, I could think about
him. I sat that morning thinking about the talks we
used to have on Saturday mornings. It would've
been nice to talk about the things that were going
right. I had worked so hard to win, and when it finally happened, Pop wasn't there to see it. So I
spent the time anyway, thinking of what I would
say to him. "We're getting good blocking on the
sweeps. We could use more time on the pass plays
and I wish the timing on the counters was better."
But he wasn't there to hear any of it.

Darrel picked me up again. He drove a lot, since

139

Mom was so busy. She said she had an appointment that day and would try to make it. She said it so quick, it made me wonder if she really did or if there were just other things she would rather do.

"Can you get a ride with Darrel?" she asked me the night before.

"Yeah, sure," I said. That was about as much as we talked then.

When we got to the field, Coach cut our warm-ups short and gathered us together in the end zone for one of his talks. As always, he fiddled with his glasses, which were falling apart. He talked about the Romans, and he talked about honor. But none of it really made sense. I think he was more nervous than we were.

The band started playing then. We didn't realize it at first; we thought they were still warming up, but then we could almost recognize a melody. We waited for the flip. Spray Can and Bam went out to midfield as the captains. We watched from the sideline. Every one of us could see the coin float through the air, catching pieces of the sun as it turned slowly and dropped to the ground.

We lost the flip and West would receive. Another bad sign.

Heat kicked it deep and it rolled into the end zone, where the return man downed it. The ball came out to the twenty and the defense—rather, Spray Can—went to work. He was everywhere. He made three unassisted tackles in the first series. We were all wondering what had gotten into him. On fourth down they punted deep and I returned it to about midfield. Maybe it wasn't as bad as it seemed.

Then our offense took the field. On the first play we lost three yards. On the second we lost seven. On the third it was another two. Heat punted on fourth down, and he barely got the ball off. Not only was Farts an open door, but the rest of the line wasn't doing much either. The whole first half we gained only seven yards. But West wasn't scoring either. So at halftime we got the "Prove it" speech again. It did help some, but we missed Taco Bell pulling ahead of the sweeps. You just gotta have that one lead block to bust it open. We figured the only thing we could do was throw the ball to keep the linebackers from crashing. I grabbed Farts by the face mask in the huddle on our first possession of the second half.

"Plug the hole," I said. "That's all you gotta do!"

He nodded his head. He was already tired. It was the most football he had played in his entire life. On first down Bam launched a deep pass. He had to rush it, so he overthrew me by five or six yards. But it worked. It spooked the defense and they adjusted to play the pass. We threw short the next play, a little slant-out to Heat, and he turned the corner for a first down. Farts was plugging the hole. Bam was getting just enough time to throw the ball. We completed one more pass before Bam threw the interception. It seems like everybody who's ever played football has one play they replay in their heads for the rest of their life. They tell it over and over to whoever will listen to it. It's the first story they tell someone they just met, and they tell it every Christmas no matter how many times it's been told before. That's how this interception will be remembered by Farts. Every time he tells it, it will get bigger and bigger until it's the only thing he remembers about football.

I ran a deep post. Heat ran a deep flag, and Flame cut across the middle. Bam fired the ball to Flame, but the middle linebacker stepped in front of him and picked off the ball and started running straight upfield. We were helpless; no one was even close. Except for Farts.

Farts got a bead on him early. The linebacker was running madly, waving the ball out in front of him like he knew he had a touchdown. He had a clear alley all the way to the goal line. He had to get by only one man, the biggest man on the field, the player who had finished dead last in the hundred-yard dash every time he had ever run it: Farts. Our whole season, everything we had hoped for, dreamed of, punished ourselves for, now rested on a kid whose only claim to fame was that he once ate eleven pies at the state fair in seven minutes.

Farts seemed the Goliath about to be humiliated by a quick-footed David. As the linebacker sped toward Farts, Farts could do only one thing: guess. He wasn't quick enough to react. To get the jump, Farts would have to guess which side the linebacker would cut to, then lunge in that direction. Somehow, we all knew this. We were frozen, watching each step as if it were in slow motion. At the last second, Farts threw his big body to the left. A good guess, since it was the linebacker's right. Most ball carriers prefer to cut right, including this linebacker. He cut at almost the exact same time Farts threw himself. When the linebacker realized his mistake, he tried to hurdle the huge mound that had rolled in front of him. But it was too late. Farts hit him in the knees and the linebacker went head over heels before slamming into the turf.

That's how the third quarter ended, all of us cheering and slapping Farts. He had saved the game. Farts had saved the game.

The fourth quarter was all defense again. Spray Can was still playing out of his head. Our offense moved the ball with the short pass, but we couldn't get another first down. The linebackers were pounding us. We couldn't move the ball on the ground, either, and our line wasn't giving Bam enough time to throw it deep. So on our last offensive possession, Coach called time-out.

"Drastic times call for drastic measures," he said. "They may be bigger and faster than we are, but they're not smarter."

Then he drew up a play that wasn't like anything we had ever seen before. He lined up the whole team on the right side of the ball. The receivers were all wide right, nearly on the sideline. When the ball was snapped, they all ran straight up the field. Bam lined up for the deep snap like we were going to punt. He'd look to the right first, then throw left. See, with everybody on the right side of the ball, that makes the center the left end; it makes him eligible as a receiver. And no one expects the center to go out for a pass. When we asked Coach about it later, he didn't say if it was legal or not, only that it was worth a try. And I guess he did it with so much confidence, the referees figured it was all by the book. We never did look it up.

Anyway, Cobra was a tall, skinny kid. He played basketball and had great hands. He made a good center because he was quick on his feet for a big kid, and he handled the ball well. His eyes lit up at the thought of scoring a touchdown. We charged out onto the field after that time-out knowing we would win the game. When we broke from the huddle and everybody lined up on the right side, it put the defense into instant confusion. They were jumping around, not knowing what to do. At the last second they all shifted to the same side of the field we were on, figuring it was a fake punt. Cobra snapped the ball. It seemed the whole world rushed to the right side of the field, except for Cobra. He ran a few steps left and Bam dumped the ball off to him before being smothered by the rushing defense. Cobra snatched it out of the air with one hand like he would a rebound and ran down the left sideline while everybody on West's team stood there wondering if we could really pass to the center. The West coach was furious. He stomped around, screaming and throwing things for the rest of the game. But it was no use. We had won. And no matter how many times the referees explained it to him, he still wouldn't believe it. We had robbed him. We had beaten his team with a second-string guard who had made a lucky guess and a backyard play drawn up in the grass that had made our center a receiver. We had snuck in as the underdog and stolen away their chance at the championship game. It wasn't football at its finest; it was desperation, it was trickery, it was brilliant. The least likely team to win a game at all had made it to the championship. It was the year of "the holy transformation," as Coach kept saying when the season was over. It was a miracle and we all knew it.

On Monday, Ed Stebbings filled up my locker with shaving cream. I didn't care. I figured it was kind of a compliment. Besides, I didn't have time to think about getting even. I spent every night that week at the hospital with my pop. I did my homework, and talked to Pop, which wasn't very often because he mostly slept. But when we did talk, it was always about the same thing: how amazing it was that we had made it to the championship game.

"You deserve it," he said to me every night with his hoarse voice. "You worked hard, you deserve it."

And every time we talked about it, I wanted to ask him the same question, but I never could. I was too afraid of what the answer might be. Finally, on Friday night, I asked him.

"Can you make it to the game, Pop?"

He didn't answer me. He just looked at me and I could see his eyes getting watery. I couldn't stand that. I couldn't stand seeing him so weak, so helpless. I needed him to be out of bed, stuffing pads in my uniform, taping my ankle, walking with me to the field and standing there on the sideline where I could get a glimpse of him between plays, standing there solid like he belonged there, like he would always be there, like nothing could move him. I hated seeing him lying there in that bed, tubes everywhere, machines keeping him alive, his voice as weak as a grandmother's.

He reached out and touched my hand, grabbed ahold of it. I wanted to leave but he wouldn't let me.

"I need you. . . ." he said.

He held on to me for a long time. I stood there being angry and sad at the same time. I had never thought my father could need me. It made me somehow feel responsible for what he was going through. I wanted to say something, I wanted to give him something. I wanted it all to be easier. But the only thing I could think to give him was a win, a championship. He deserved it more than I did.

When I got home that night, Leisl was at my house. I couldn't talk to her very long because I was due at Spray Can's. That night was the biggest territory-marking ritual of the year. We were playing the championship game at the university. There would be bleachers, benches for players, a place for the band, and even a trainer. But it also meant that we had to sneak past the security guards the night before, get onto the field to mark both end zones, then get out of there without getting caught. We were afraid that if one of us got busted, he wouldn't be allowed to play. But we were more afraid of what would happen if we didn't call on the forces of nature for the biggest game of the season.

So I didn't spend much time with Leisl. I guess I wish I had. Because I miss her now, and that's not something you can make up for.

"I'm leaving after the game," she said to me. "I was supposed to leave last week, but I wanted to see you win one more time."

"Maybe we won't win," I said.

"You will," she said. "I know it."

Then she showed me the bottle cap from our football lessons. She had tied it on a string and hung it from her neck.

"For good luck," she said. "Just in case."

"Won't I see you after the game?" I asked her.

"You'll be celebrating with Taco Bell and Heater," she said back.

"Heat," I said. And I realized she was right. We had all worked hard together, and for better or worse we would be together after the game.

"Besides, she said. "My plane leaves at two. I'll just have time to get there."

"I wish you could stay longer," I said before I realized I had said it.

She smiled and said, "It's okay to feel alone."

When I looked at her, I knew she understood. She had been away from her parents for three months. And even though she was going back, she knew what it was like to be without them.

"Yes, well," I said. "I guess I don't have a choice."

"The angry one," she said, then kissed me on the cheek. "I will miss you."

Then she held the bottle cap in her hand.

"Good luck," she said. And walked away.

I stood on my front porch for a long time staring after her. She had given me my first kiss, and even though it was on the cheek, it was one I would never forget.

When I was about to step off the stairs and jog to Spray Can's, an old plumber's van pulled up in front of my house. I read the slogan on the driver's door. MAXFIELD PLUMBING, it said. *Call us first when you've got a leak.*

I looked at the driver and it was Spray Can. I started to laugh.

"What are you doin'?" I shouted to him.

"You the one with a leak?" he said.

"Yeah," I said, running toward him. "Let's get out of here before my mom sees you driving."

I climbed in the passenger side and found the rest of the team in the back, including Heat's dogs.

"This will work," I said to Spray Can.

"You bet it will," he said back, and everybody laughed.

"I got doughnuts!" I heard someone yell. I turned back around and saw Taco Bell's scabbed face smiling big in the darkness.

"All right," I yelled. "Taco Bell is back!"

Everybody cheered and we drove to the university like we owned the town. Then we drove around the stadium, just to get a look at it. Even though the lights weren't on, we could see them standing like centurions, their heads disappearing into the night clouds.

"Wow!" Taco Bell kept saying. "Wow!"

We parked the van next to the fence so we could hop on it to climb over. Then we ran onto the field to throw the football in the dark. We couldn't get enough of the place. We had to see everything. Where the players drank their water, where they sat, where they huddled on the sideline around their coach to talk about new plays, new blocking assignments. We were like grave robbers in the great pyramid, touching everything, looking for something to take home, some memento, something that would give us good luck for the next day's game. Most guys found bits of tape or pages from programs. But I scored the biggest when I found a chin strap.

"It's a sign," Taco Bell said.

I held the chin strap above my head.

"Is it a good sign or a bad sign?" I asked him.

Everybody was quiet; then Taco Bell spoke up.

"It's a good sign!"

We all cheered and danced like warriors. Heat's dogs howled at us and we knew the force of nature was strong. We ran to the first end zone and marked it. Then we chanted and ran to the other end zone and marked it.

That's when the flashlight hit us.

"What's going on here?" we heard a voice yell at us.

We were running before we had our pants zipped up. More than one player yelped, having panicked and zipped up too soon. We ran as fast as we could to the fence and piled over onto the roof of the van. It wasn't until we were all inside that I realized I had dropped the lucky chin strap. Spray Can fired up the van.

"Wait!" I shouted. "I dropped the chin strap!"

Before I could scale the fence, Heat sent one of his dogs after it.

"Fetch!" was all he said, and pointed to the chin strap.

The dog clawed under the fence through a hole

152 | T<small>HE</small> H<small>EARTBEAT OF</small> H<small>ALFTIME</small>

and bounded after the chin strap. The flashlight was headed in the same direction. We heard the guard scream in fear; then the flashlight fell to the ground and went out. Heat's dog was back in a matter of seconds with the chin strap in his mouth. We could hear the guard cussing and looking for his flashlight as we drove away. The football gods were watching over us.

THE CHAMPIONSHIP GAME

was awake long before my alarm went off the next morning. I couldn't sleep that night and spent most of it staring at the ceiling in my room. It was too cold to sit on the roof, so I just lay there, staring, thinking, not thinking. Everything I've told you so far went through my head. That's when I decided to write it down, that night when it all kept filling up my head so I couldn't sleep. I figured if I didn't write it down someplace, I'd never sleep again. I wrote on all the bits of paper I could find, writing everything I could think of on scraps that looked like some great puzzle laid out all over the floor of my room. Then I gathered them all up and stuffed them in my closet, where I would get to them sometime later, long after the game was over and I could sit with Spray Can and make sense of it all.

When the sun was finally up, I sat in the middle of the floor with all my pads and slowly got dressed. Once again I was preparing for battle. I had my armor, and I had the spirit of my father sitting beside me. I talked to him about the game, about every play, every detail of each assignment. I talked about pass patterns, how soon to cut in on a man, how to brush him off, turn him around, outrun him. I talked about blocking, keeping my head up, my feet moving. I talked about running the ball, cutting back against the grain, turning the corner on the sweeps, getting the extra yard.

When all the pads were in, and I had everything on but my helmet, I stood in the middle of the room.

"See you at the game," I said to my father. And I had this strange feeling that he'd heard me.

I went downstairs and Mom had breakfast for me.

"You're up early," I said to her. "I mean for a Saturday."

"I wouldn't miss this game for anything," she said.

That surprised me. She had always hated football. Every season she would get upset that I was even playing; then she and Pop would argue about it for a while.

"I thought you didn't like football," I said.

"I don't," she said. "But I like you. . . . Here's your breakfast."

"Thanks," I said.

She smiled at me. Seemed like it had been such a long time that she had smiled or been happy with something. I think about it now, and maybe she realized that before long it was going to be just me and her; and that maybe she better start getting used to it. Including the football.

Mom sat next to me while I ate. After a moment, she spoke to me.

"I love him too, you know," she said.

I nodded my head, not knowing what to say.

We sat alone like that for a time, not talking, just sitting. Still, it was a good beginning.

As always, I was the first one to the field. Mom dropped me off at the players' entrance, then went to find herself a good seat. I didn't see anyone there when I jogged out onto the field to warm up. The stadium was a lot bigger in the daytime. I looked at the fence where we had climbed over the night before. I laughed to myself thinking about the security guard being scared out of his pants when he caught sight of Heat's dog charging toward him. Then I thought about the chin strap. I pulled my helmet on to make sure the chin strap fit. It did, and I rubbed it for good luck.

That's when I saw Coach sitting on one of the benches on the sideline.

"It's a big place, isn't it?" he asked me without getting up.

"Yes," I said loudly, since I was standing so far away from him. I couldn't think of anything else to say. I had never been alone with Coach before. And even though we had spent a whole season together, it seemed like I didn't know him at all. I walked over and sat beside him.

"You know," he said. "One of the main reasons we're sitting right here today is because of the way you've played this season."

"Thanks," I said.

"Everyone tells me this is the best season you've ever had. I don't know, this is my first year in this league, in this town. But that's what they tell me. Is it true?"

"I guess so."

"Why do you suppose that is?" he asked me.

"I don't know," I said.

"We never know, do we?" he said.

It was the first thing anybody had said to me that really made sense. That was it. We don't know why things happen, or what's going to happen. There are a lot of things we just can't do anything about. And there are a lot of things we're never going to understand. That's life. No sense being angry at what you can't change. You just find a way to make the most of it, to make it work.

We both looked at the sun over the stadium then. It was cold, but it was a clear morning. A perfect day for football.

"Let's win us a game today," Coach said.

Sitting there with him, I believed we would.

Shortly after that, everyone else arrived. We went through warm-ups at one end of the field while Cyprus warmed up at the other end. There were people slowly moving into the stadium, and we all knew they would never fill it. Not for this game. I think we all dreamed of a packed stadium, but we weren't disappointed when only the first few rows filled up. The last to arrive was the band. Just as we were going into the locker room for a five-minute pep talk, the band hurried into the seats behind the end zone. As we ran by, they all held out their gloved hands to slap us five and shout to us.

"You're the best!" they yelled.

"So are you guys!" Taco Bell shouted back.

I guess he was just caught up in all the excitement and couldn't think of anything else to say. We could hear the band warm up as we made our way through the tunnel and into the locker room. Most of the team was too awestruck to hear what Coach was saying. It was the biggest day in all of our lives. It would be tough to concentrate before the game. Coach knew this, so he didn't say much.

"We have a win waiting for us," he said. "There's a championship right here. By lunchtime today you could be champions. You all deserve it. You deserve it more than anyone on that Cyprus team. You've had more to overcome. More to prove. More to lose."

He looked at me then, understanding what had motivated me all season.

"Now," he continued. "Let's go have some fun. Let's go win us a football game!"

We all yelled then, and gathered into a huddle around Coach.

"You want to win this game?" he shouted at us.

"Yes!" we shouted back.

"Then let's go prove it!" he yelled.

We all screamed like infantrymen and stormed the field. Cyprus had already done its screaming and was on the opposite sideline. They watched us jump into each other, yelling and smacking helmets. For the first time all year we recognized what the band was playing. It was our school song. We cheered as half the audience sang along. I turned and looked into the stands while Heat and Spray Can walked out onto the field for the flip. Even though the stands were far less than half full, there were still more people at this game than I had ever seen. Then I saw Leisl. She was up front, leaning over the rail with Katie. She had the bottle-cap necklace in her hand and was looking for me. She caught sight of me and I smiled at her. She smiled back and tugged at the necklace. My cheek suddenly felt warm.

I turned back to Heat and Spray Can just in time

to see us win the flip. We would receive. The game had started and everything would fade away, the stadium, all the fans, the band. Everything except the game. It was all that mattered. I took my place on the field and waited. I could hear my own breathing. I could feel my heartbeat. I glanced at the sideline like I always do, looking for my father. He wasn't there and I grew angry again.

The whistle blew and the referee signaled for the kickoff. It was like the beginning of my life, it was like I was born right then. I heard the thud of a ball being kicked. I watched it loft over the front line, end over end, arcing first high, then down, down into my arms. I heard Heat running toward me.

"Up the middle!" he shouted, and cut in front of me to lead the blocking.

I caught up with him quickly. We were running in the same steps, pumping the same rhythm like we were on a tandem bicycle. Taco Bell laid down the first block, but the line closed in on us. Heat opened up a small gap, but it slammed in on me. I got hit hard from the left side, then the right. I lost Heat, and tried to take one more step, get one more yard. But I got hit head on. I was knocked to the ground and smothered by the defense.

When I found my way out of the tangle of bodies, my left hand was numb. It felt like it had been cut off. I tried to find my way back to the huddle, but it hurt so bad I had to stop. The referee called time-out and one of the college trainers ran onto the field.

"Where does it hurt?" he asked me.

"My hand," I said painfully. "I took a helmet in the hand."

As I walked off the field, I turned around to see Heat growing angry. I had made it to about the thirty yard line. But without me, Stones would have to play halfback. Stones was not fast enough to be a threat on the sweeps or the passes. He played defense and we brought him in on offense only when we had to play power football.

"Heat is going to have a long game if I don't get back out there," I said to myself.

So while the trainer iced my hand and checked for broken bones, Heat ran the dive, play after play. Stones was a pretty good blocker, and our line was angry enough to hit hard. Heat was gaining four or five yards a play. Taco Bell was playing like a madman. You could see the scabs on his face, and after a few plays they got knocked loose and started to bleed. The scabs on his elbow and leg were bleeding too. He looked like a psycho soldier. I think it scared the other team half to death. Taco Bell knew it and played it up. He'd growl and yell like an ax murderer, then wipe blood on his pants. The kid he was blocking got so intimidated, he wouldn't even line up in front of Taco Bell; he played back, off the line.

Bam just kept handing off to Heat behind Stones

and they ran to Taco Bell's side all the way to the end zone. By the time they got there, nearly every player on the defense had blood on his jersey from a Taco Bell block. Heat punched in the extra point, and we were up 7 to 0.

Cyprus had come all the way to that stadium to win back what they thought was theirs. They showed up to redeem themselves, to teach us a lesson. What they found was a blood-covered crazyman who chopped up their defense like cordwood. They were stunned at the first score.

We kicked off, and Cyprus met psycho number two, Spray Can. At the last minute, Ray showed up at the game. I swear you could smell him. That odor of gasoline and grease swept through the stadium. Spray Can caught the smell and it made him crazy, it reminded him of what it was he was trying to prove. He played every minute of that game at full speed. He made the tackle on the kickoff. He blitzed on the first play and hit the fullback head-on two yards behind the line of scrimmage. He collapsed the corner on the sweep the next play and took two blockers with him before colliding with the halfback. Cyprus tried one more play, this one away from Spray Can, but they gained only a yard and had to punt on the next down. They were totally confused.

"Somebody block him!" the quarterback yelled, pointing at Spray Can.

Spray Can just smiled. Nobody could stop him, and he knew it.

Our offense took the field just as the trainer was telling me I had broken a bone in my hand. He was poking at a lump behind my knuckles and I turned away because it hurt. I looked downfield at the gate we had climbed and was thinking about our ritual the night before. Then I saw Darrel walking in slowly, pushing something. I looked closer. It was a wheelchair he was pushing, it was my father in a wheelchair.

"Tape it," I said to the trainer.

"What?" he answered.

"Tape it," I yelled at him.

"Okay," he said.

First he taped my hand so it couldn't move.

"Leave my thumb out so I can catch," I said to him.

He just shook his head and did what I told him. And while he taped, I watched my father. He hardly moved. Darrel wheeled him up to the corner of the end zone and made sure he was warm. He tucked the blanket tightly around him. Then he disappeared for a moment, and returned with a chair so he could sit with my father. They sat there, the two of them, seeming so different. Darrel so big and strong. No worries, just a whole life ahead of him. And my father, withered and having only a few days left in a life that had been long and hard.

Heat and Stones put on another good show, but it wasn't enough and we had to punt before we got to midfield. So while Spray Can confused and destroyed their offense again, the trainer finished taping my hand. It looked like a big club. He had taped it tight so that it wouldn't move; then he taped a pad on it so I wouldn't hurt it again. By the time Cyprus was punting the ball, I was standing next to Coach. He looked at me, wondering what I was doing. I don't think he planned on seeing me the rest of the game. Then he smiled.

"It's about time," he said.

I ran onto the field for the next offensive series. Bam looked at me in the huddle and said, "All right . . . *bam!* . . . let's mix it up."

He threw me the pitch the first play and I had to catch it with one hand. I turned the corner before the safety could crash in on me to force me out of bounds. I gained eleven yards. The next play Bam ran was brilliant. Fake to me on the sweep and hand off to Heat on the counter. Heat gained sixteen or so yards and we were past midfield.

"Throw me the ball," I said to Bam in the huddle.

"It's first down," he said. "And you only got one hand."

"Just throw it," I said.

"Okay," Bam said, and he called flare pass right.

I lined up behind the tight end and ran the perfect flare to the outside. I had the cornerback beat by a couple steps and Bam delivered the ball the way he had a thousand times before in practice. But when I turned to make the catch, I realized I was looking over my right shoulder, making my club hand the outside hand. So to catch the ball, I had to almost backhand it with my right. The ball hit my right hand, then the club, then dropped away from me onto the turf. I dove to the ground trying to make the catch, but it was no use. When I got up, I saw Darrel.

"Run it to the inside," he shouted at me. Then he turned and showed me with his right hand how I would make the catch. I looked at my father, and even though he didn't move, I could tell it was what he was thinking too. I ran back to the huddle.

"Run it to the inside," I said to Bam. "Run the post."

"No," Bam said.

"I can get it," I said.

"Thirty-one dive," Bam said. "On two."

Heat gained a few yards. Then a few more the next play. But it wasn't enough for the first down. Cyprus was on to us. They shut down the ends and we had to punt. It didn't seem right. We moved the ball so easily, then hit the wall. That's how it went until halftime. Neither team doing much until time was nearly out. On their last series of the half, Cyprus crossed the two wide receivers about mid-field and their quarterback launched a desperation pass to keep them in the game. Sparky cut in front of the receiver, jumped up, and got a hand on the ball to flutter the flight. But the receiver slowed and scooped the ball up before it hit the ground, and while our whole team watched in disbelief, he ran to the end zone. We were shell-shocked, and didn't try all that hard to prevent their extra point attempt. Their big fullback ran right up the middle while we stood around wondering how that kid made the catch.

Score at halftime: 7 each.

"Ulysses had a vision," Coach said to us in the locker room. "A vision of a distant land, a land he believed was his."

We all knew Ulysses from Coach's talks earlier in the year. We knew he had completed nearly impossible tasks.

"We have our own vision," Coach continued. "This is our football game. This is our territory. We have laid claim to it, marked each end zone."

Our faces lit up. He knew about our ritual. And he'd said "we." Did that mean he too had marked the end zone? Could that have been him with the flashlight last night? As the mystery grew, so did our passion for victory.

"This is our football field," he yelled. "Ours by every natural and god-given right!"

We went crazy, yelling and screaming.

"No one can take it away from us! No one!"

The roar was so loud it made our heads ring, ring with adrenaline.

"Now let's go get what belongs to us!"

We charged the field even crazier than we had the first half. Cyprus must've been wondering what it was that could get us so psyched up for a game. But we knew. It was three years of losing, it was feeling alone in your own school, your own family. It wasn't about winning. It was about never wanting to lose anything again. Cyprus had never felt that. They had never sat together as a team after losing so badly it made them wonder if they would ever play football again.

We kicked off the second half, and Cyprus lost more yards than they gained. They were bigger than we were. They were faster. But they could not move the ball. When the fullback broke one loose up the middle, little Sparky stood him up with a hit so hard it staggered him and he fell over on his side. Our defense exploded. Our smallest man, our free safety, had taken on their huge fullback and rocked him right down to his toenails. There wasn't anything Cyprus could do to get past our howling defense.

When our offense took the field, we moved forty yards in three plays. The sweep. The counter. The dive. Everything worked. Taco Bell had dried blood all over his face and no one would go near him. He had to chase people down to block them. But the drive ended on the two yard line when we ran the sweep and I fumbled just before stepping into the end zone. I walked to the sideline without ever looking up. We had the win, we had the momentum. And I'd handed it to Cyprus without a fight, like handing over my wallet to a gang of thugs. I couldn't believe it, and I couldn't look at my father. All I could think of was him going back to the hospital with this vision of his son giving away the championship. His last football memory would be of his son fumbling on the two yard line.

The fumble gave Cyprus new life, it gave them all the energy we had. They moved the ball slowly upfield against our dejected defense. Time was running out. Cyprus had control of the game. A score seemed inevitable.

"Suck it up!" we yelled from the sideline. But it didn't do any good. Cyprus had a first down with four minutes left, and they were inside the twenty yard line. Their huge center was getting a good piece of Spray Can every play and they were gaining four yards a carry. That's when Spray Can called time-out. He huddled up the defense and drew a play in the grass. When they came back to the line, Sparky was playing noseguard. Smallest guy on the team, and Spray Can sticks him at noseguard! Before Coach could do anything about it, Cyprus was over the ball. We heard the cadence. We watched the center lift and hike the ball. Then, with incredible speed, Sparky shot between the center's legs and got ahold of the quarterback's ankles before he could hand the ball off.

The sideline went crazy. For the first time in the drive, Cyprus lost yards. They lined up again. Sparky took on the center again. This time when the center hiked the ball, he flattened out and lay on Sparky. Not a bad idea, except that Spray Can crashed the line right behind Sparky, and with the center lying down, it was an easy hurdle for Spray Can. He jumped the two like he was striding over a hay bale, then ran down the halfback, who was headed for the corner on a sweep. The sideline erupted again. Now it was third down and twenty yards to go for a first down. The defense had backed them up ten yards in two plays. We were all screaming, but above it all we could hear Ray cheering for his son.

"Yeah!" he'd yell. "That's it, yeah!"

It was the most any of us had ever heard him say.

When Cyprus lined up again, we all knew what the play was. Pass. Sparky had moved back to safety, and our linebackers covered the flats. The quarterback set up, but no one was open and he threw the ball out of bounds. On fourth down they tried the screen pass, but the halfback gained only four yards against a pumped-up defense that read the play perfectly. Spray Can's smarts had saved the game, and with just under a minute left, Bam led us out onto the field.

We ran a counter first, then a sweep, figuring they were expecting a pass. That put us at about midfield with a first down. We had time for maybe two more plays. Trouble was, Heat was breathin' hard. He had taken a shot in the ribs and was having a hard time catching his breath.

I looked over at my father. He still hadn't moved much, only adjusted his arms a little.

"Run it to the inside!" I heard Darrel yelling.

Bam called sweep left. I got only about four yards before the linebacker drilled me and knocked the ball loose. I just couldn't hang on to the ball with my club hand, and I watched it bounce slowly away from me while nearly every Cyprus player on the field went after it. The ball bounced out of bounds. The gods were with us. We had one play left. One play to go home champions.

"Run the post," I said to Bam when we were in the huddle. "I can catch to the inside."

Bam called time-out. Coach came out and looked at his two backs. Then he sent for the fastest guys on the team.

"They know it's going to be a pass," he said. "We might as well throw our fastest guys at them."

Then he drew deep pass patterns in the grass, criss-crossing the middle and all ending up in the end zone.

"Look for Flame," he said as he walked off the field.

Bam looked at me, then at Flame.

"Get open," he said to Flame. "Everybody else run like you're about to get six."

I lined up wide, just outside the end. I looked at the linebacker as if I was coming his way. The safety picked up on it and cheated in. When the ball was snapped, the safety dropped back and so did the linebackers. Only four defensive men rushed. Bam had plenty of time to throw the ball, but everyone was covered. Everyone but me. I guess the D-backs figured that after two fumbles and a dropped pass, we'd never throw up a forty-yard pass to a receiver with a club hand. They were wrong. As I bent my route to the inside, I saw that I was open. I saw Bam look left, then right, trying to find a receiver. Then he caught sight of me—all alone, headed for the end zone. I was his only hope. He launched a spiral nearly into the clouds. It was high, and far. I knew by the arc that he'd given it everything he had, closed his eyes and just heaved it. I ran under the ball, watching it turn. I crossed the goal line and reached up with one hand. This time there was no club hand in the way, there was no linebacker to knock it loose, not even a resting clarinet player to trip me up. I caught the ball the way I would have in my front yard, easily, with one hand pulling it in like I was pulling a pear off a tree. For a moment I was crossing my own driveway, gliding across the same grass I mowed every Saturday afternoon, catching passes my father tossed after work. I curled my arm around the ball, drew it into my chest like the head of a friend or a little brother. It was as if it belonged there, like I could've closed my eyes and called to it and it would be there, nested in my arms. Then I heard my father calling to me from the driveway.

"Nice catch!"

And suddenly he was there, we were there, at the championship game, in the end zone together, listening to the roar of the crowd, the thunder of my teammates behind me. In a moment I would be smothered by them.

I flipped the ball to my father. It floated slowly through the air, and with every spin I could see my father as a young man running downfield, waiting for the pass to drop out of the sky, running in his own days of glory. I could see his eyes watching the ball, his hands reaching, reaching out to me as I learned to walk, wrapping around my own hands while I grew. I could see him go off in the morning to a job he hated, wanting to be home, throwing a football with his son. And I realized that I wasn't angry anymore, that we all have our day, that some are shorter than others, that there are moments we remember forever: the way a football feels in your hands, the way a certain girl holds a bottle cap or leaves your cheek warm with a kiss, the way a friend sprays out the words "Sthee you around," the way your father waits for you by the window, waits to see you one more time before he's gone, leaving you nothing but his heartbeat in your own chest pounding out the uncertainty of the future and the memories of the past.

The ball dropped into my father's hands and he cradled it like a baby. Was it me? Was he remembering too? I didn't know how much longer he would live then, and suddenly it didn't matter. I had his heart. And I would listen to it for the rest of my life.

WE ARE THE CHAMPIONS

When we got to the lunchroom on Monday, the band had lined up all around the room and was playing the school song. It was as if they knew what was about to happen. The music was as bad as it ever was, but we were enjoying it. It was ours, and we were proud of it, even if we couldn't recognize enough of the notes to sing along. That's when Ed Stebbings and his gang walked into the room. They made it clear why they were there, as if we didn't know already. They showed up at school that day with only one thing on their minds: destroy any celebration we had planned.

"You're still a bunch of losers," Ed shouted at me.

The whole room went silent. I admit, I was a little nervous. I wasn't afraid of Ed; I guess I just wasn't sure what I would do. I knew it was coming, I had known all season that Fat Ed with the rancid breath would one day force a showdown with me. It was the sort of showdown you see in bad Westerns. We stood there, face-to-face, staring at each other with steely eyes. Ed even had his arms bent a little, like he was about to draw. There must've been a hundred kids standing there waiting. Ed had said his piece, and now it was up to me to respond. For that split second I thought about the season we had had. I think I finally realized what we had accomplished. For a moment, a very brief moment, I loved the world. I wanted to stick out my hand and say to Ed, "Let's put everything aside, huh, pal? Why don't we all just be friends." Then I saw myself shake his hand and everybody cheer while we all celebrated. I kinda wish that's how it happened. But Ed wouldn't have it that way. He slapped the milk out of my hand and growled at me.

I stood my ground.

"You're the loser, Ed," I said to him.

There was a short pause, like everyone was taking one last breath before the world ended; then the lunchroom exploded into the biggest food riot the universe has ever known. The band came to their senses quickly and started playing to cover up the noise of the confrontation. Some of them even locked the doors, except for the door that went outside. Fats was standing there with his tuba, and he pushed the door open to let Heat's dogs in. The dogs charged into the crowd like wild boars and people started going down with the wind knocked out of 'em. The crotch attack was deadly. Somehow the dogs knew who the enemy was. When one would go down, we'd charge with lunch trays and smother the victim with creamed corn and sticky pudding. Spray Can was always first on the scene with a tray full of pig food. He'd launch it sidearm and strafe the downed man with slop. He'd celebrate briefly, then scream, "Reload! Reload!"

It was like Custer's Last Stand; Stebbings in the middle and a clan of crazed warriors closing in on him, redeeming their tribe for all the injustice he had rained on them over the years. Before long, teachers were pounding on the doors, trying to get in. But the band played on, and the janitor stood in the corner, not making a move to try and stop the whole thing. Taco Bell was shouting "Charge!" and the whole place soon looked like the inside of a disposal. There was food everywhere. One of the worst hit was Fats. I guess his tuba was the easiest target, and in a matter of minutes it was full of Jell-O lumps and chicken wings. Stebbings and his boys lost ground quickly. They tried to make a break for one of the doors, but Taco Bell read their play perfectly and pounded the first two escapees to the ground with a textbook block. They were soon smothered in slop, and Taco Bell was soon smothered by Katie.

You kind of expect a first kiss to be under romantic conditions. But there was Taco Bell, covered in creamed corn and Jell-O, and Katie kissing him all over the face like he was a war hero. When she let him up for air, he screamed and celebrated like he'd just won the doughnut lottery.

I got to admire ol' Stebbings. He put up a good fight. Soon as he was knocked down, he was up quick and running hard toward another exit. He put his head down and charged the line of band members like a pulling guard. But Spray Can stepped in front of the band and hit the red-haired bully with a perfect tackle, knocking him over the top of a table and right onto his back. It would've been good for Ed if we had stopped there. But we didn't. Ed Stebbings, that legendary, red-haired bully with the dog breath, had thrown his weight around one too many times. Before he could get to his feet, the mob had picked him up and was rushing him toward the worst possible punishment any of us could think of, that sickening pile of stink, that vomit bucket, that barrel of barf . . . the wet-garbage can! He slid in easily, like a ball through a hoop, headfirst, all the way up to his ankles. The mob cheered like they had just saved the village from a werewolf; then they picked up the garbage can, Ed and all, and tossed the whole thing outside. Ed spilled out and just sat there, horrified and covered with wet stinky garbage.

That's when the principal wrenched the door open, his keys still jangling from the lock. The crowd turned to silence as quickly as it had erupted into chaos.

"What in the world is going on here?" the principal shouted. Then he turned to us, and struggling to get control of his temper, he asked: "What are you trying to prove?"

No one said a word. We all had answers of our own. And they would stay that way—our own. No one could take them away. We held our heads up proudly. It was the last time we stood as a team, but we would never forget how far we had gotten together, how much we depended on each other that year. We learned that nobody could do it alone, you had to have a team; and that no matter how tough it got, you could do anything so long as you stuck together.

The principal waited for us to say something. It was perfectly silent except for the sound of a dog peeing on the side of a pop machine. It was our sound, the sound of another territory being marked, another victory. The lunchroom was ours! We would never be losers again. We had conquered the unconquerable, we had won at unbeatable odds. It was a miracle. It was the year the football gods parted the universe to give us a glimpse of the heavens. It was the autumn of 1972.